PUFFIN BOOKS

Shadow in Hawthorn Bay

One spring morning in 1815, in the highlands of Scotland where spirits and witches are a fact of life and the ancient feast of Beltane is still celebrated, fifteen-year-old Mary Urquhart hears her beloved cousin Duncan calling her to join him — from three thousand miles away in Upper Canada. Yet his call is so urgent that Mary sets off alone across the ocean to find him, braving the sea-voyage to Quebec, and making her way up the St. Lawrence until she finally comes to Hawthorn Bay on Lake Ontario — only to discover that Duncan is dead, and that her aunt and uncle have moved on.

Mary is not just alone in this frightening land of primeval forests — she is also misunderstood by the practical Yankees who have settled in the district, and who distrust her powers of "second sight" and her Gaelic belief in ghosts and witches. For despite Duncan's death, Mary still hears his voice calling her to join him. But as she battles threatening dark forces and fights for her survival, Mary unexpectedly finds friendship — with cheerful Patty and little Henry, with Owena, the quiet Indian who recognizes the healing powers in her, and with Luke — so very different from "Duncan the black".

Shadow in Hawthorn Bay is an enthralling historical tale of mystery and love.

N

Our House

Hawthorn Bay

Collivers' Cors

The Island

Kingston

Soames

Lake Ontario

Shadow in Hawthorn Bay

St. Lawrence River · Prescott · Rapids · Cornwall · Montréal

JANET LUNN

Puffin Books

PUFFIN BOOKS

Published by the Penguin Group
Penguin Books Canada Ltd., 2801 John Street,
Markham, Ontario, Canada L3R 1B4
Penguin Books, 27 Wrights Lane, London W8 5TZ, England
Viking Penguin Inc., 40 West 23rd Street,
New York, New York 10010, USA
Penguin Books Australia Ltd., Ringwood,
Victoria, Australia
Penguin Books (NZ) Ltd., 182-190 Wairau Road,
Auckland 10, New Zealand

Penguin Books Ltd., Registered Offices:
Harmondsworth, Middlesex, England

First published by Lester & Orpen Dennys Limited, 1986
Published in Puffin Books, 1988

Frontispiece map by Jonathan Gladstone, j.b. geographics
Chapter opening illustration by Amanda Duffy

Manufactured in Canada by Gagne Printing Ltd.

Canadian Cataloguing in Publication Data

Lunn, Janet, 1928-
  Shadow in Hawthorn Bay

ISBN 0-14-032436-4

I. Title.

PS8573.U55S54 1988   jC813'.54   C87-094823-7
PZ7.L85Sh 1988

This book is for Jean,
with love

Grateful acknowledgements to:

The Canada Council and the Ontario Arts Council for
financial assistance;

Mollie Hunter and Michael McIlwraith, Invernesshire, for
their generous hospitality and advice;

Dorothy Davies, Trenton Ontario Memorial Library, for her
helpful assistance;

Edith Fowke, for kindly opening her music library;

Jessica Latshaw, Joyce Barkhouse, and my family for having
faith in this story over a long period of time;

Edward Lukeman for Davie Cameron's map;

Louise Dennys, my editor, for her clear good sense, endless
patience, and encouragement.

Glossary of Gaelic terms

an dà shelladh — the second sight

beannachd Dhé leat — may the blessing of God attend you

bodach — brownie, hobgoblin

coire na cailleach — hag's cave

Dia — God

dubh — black

feasd, am feasd — never

glaistig — female fairy, ghost

iùilas — spells

mo gràdach — my dear one

och-on — alas

sitheachean — fairies

slan leat — greetings

taibhes — a vision of the second sight

tigh na shuidh — the house on the resting-place

tornashee (literally tor-na-sitheachean) the fairies' hill

uan — lamb

Sources: The New English-Gaelic Dictionary compiled by Derick Thomson (Gairm Publications, Glasgow, 1981); Gaelic Dictionary compiled by Malcolm Mackinnon (ACAIR and Aberdeen University Press, first pub. 1925, reprinted 1984).

CHAPTER I
Come, Mairi!

"Come, Mairi! Come you here!"

"Duncan, I cannot! Here is the lamb making sore trouble getting itself into the world. Come you to me!"

Mary went back to her work. Swiftly she turned and tugged the struggling lamb, crooning softly all the while, until, with a cry of triumph, she held it firmly in her two hands.

"There now, Sally, there is your wee *uan*," she murmured. She laid the lamb beside its mother. It began at once to suckle. Gently stroking the ewe's still heaving sides, Mary sat back on her heels, tossed her thick black hair from her sweaty face, and watched with satisfaction as the ewe began to clean her baby. Only then did she realize that Duncan had not called from the other side of the hill. He was three thousand miles away in Upper Canada. Yet he had called! Sudden tears prickled her eyes. In four years it was the first time she had heard his voice. He had sworn so often they could never be parted in life or death but he had gone away. And barely a word since.

"While you are gone," she had said, "we will still be together, Duncan. Our thoughts will travel the miles. And you will be soon home." Mary had never doubted that. She and Duncan had always been like one person, two halves of a whole. Cousins, they might as well have been twins, they had been so inseparable—until Uncle Davie and Aunt Jean had decided to leave the Highlands. Over the plaintive cry of the lapwings, the chirping of the thrushes, and the ewe and her baby bleating softly at one another, she heard Duncan's voice again, "Come, Mairi!" In it there was a note of such pain, such urgency, she could feel the sharpness of it in her own breast.

"How can I?" she cried aloud. "How can I?"

"Was you wanting help with the ewe, Mairi?" Annie Morrison called from across the field.

"I was not."

"Come away then, it is dinner time."

"In a minute." Mary rested on her heels, pulling her plaid around her against the chill April wind and fine rain. She looked down the green slope over the valley and the hills beyond, remembering the day Duncan had left the glen. Everyone in the township had gone down to the wide path by Loch Ness to see them off. The sun was shining on their six dark heads—Uncle Davie, Aunt Jean, Callum, the

2

baby, Iain, and Duncan. Standing beside the cart that held the few Cameron possessions they would take with them, tears large in his black eyes, Duncan had promised, "I will come home, Mairi. Next year I will be twelve, I will be soon grown, and I will earn the money to come home."

But it had been four years and the only word he had ever sent was a brief letter in English, not in the Gaelic they all spoke, a letter enclosed in one of Uncle Davie's a year after they had gone away.

> Upper Canada
> near the settlement of
> Collivers' Corners
> 10th day of July, 1812
>
> Dear Mary,
> Here the land is low and dark with forest.
> We are expected to make crofts of it.
> Respectfully,
> your cousin,
> Duncan Cameron

Mary hated it. And she had every word memorized. There was nothing in it of the Duncan she knew, of what he was feeling—beyond those mournful words "dark with forest"—and there was nothing in it of plans to come home. There had been letters from Uncle Davie and Aunt Jean to Mary's mother and father, letters to say that life was hard but good in Upper Canada, letters urging them to emigrate. But although she had written and written to him, there had never been another letter from Duncan, nor any sign at all.

"Four years," Mary thought bitterly. "Four years and the two of us fifteen years old already. Is it not old enough to be earning the passage home? And now you call me to come to you. Och, Duncan, you know I cannot do that."

Returning to the present, Mary gave the ewe a final loving pat and rose to her feet. Absently she crossed the field to eat her bannock and her bit of cheese with the other young herders who had gathered in the lee of the hill.

The talk was all of May Morning, the big spring festival only a week away.

"And Mairi, you will have your rowan wreath and your May Morning fire made, and your bannock rolled down the hill, and you be halfway up Clachan Mountain before the rest of us are out from our beds," laughed Jenny Macintyre.

"And I wonder do you ever go to bed at all before May Morning?" sighed Callum Grant.

"I would be a bent old woman did I wait for you to rise, Callum Grant," retorted Mary.

The others laughed, full of the joy of summer coming. The first of May was Beltane, the ancient festival with its ritual fires on every hilltop, its bannock rolling, and the herding of cows and sheep and goats up into fresh pastures in the high hills. There the women and young people would stay in their shielings, the little rough mountain huts, all summer while the men farmed in the lower hills. In the autumn they would trek home again, people and animals fat and happy.

The chatter went on but Duncan's call and the terrible need in it were so powerful that Mary got suddenly to her feet and, without a word, left the group. The others took little notice. They were used to Mary's abrupt ways.

All that afternoon, the echo of Duncan's voice was strong in her head. Over and over she relived their childhood together.

Born in the same week, they had understood one another from the first with hardly a word having to be spoken. Almost as soon as they could walk, the two had gone racing over the hills together until the rocks, the deep corries, and the swift-flowing burns had become more home to them than the hearth in either of their houses. They were so in tune that Mary's mother called them reflections of one another. "And who is to say which is the child and which the shade?" Aunt Jean would ask—and there seemed to be no answer.

They were both small, black-haired, and dark-eyed, but Duncan's eyes were large and black as sloes and people called him beautiful with his hair curling around his ruddy complexion, and his straight nose and full mouth. Mary's eyes were bright as a blackbird's, and she was plain and sharp-nosed, with skin as pale as yarrow and a mouth that turned up noticeably at one corner when she was amused. They shared an intensity and a streak of wild joy that, in Mary, though she was a solemn child, sometimes erupted in a song that was clearer than a bird's. Duncan's way was to laugh and dance, and sometimes he fluted on a whistle he made from a willow twig.

Mary had, too, both a sweetness and a "tongue sharp as a thorn", said her sister Jeannie. It showed itself in quick, sometimes unkind words. In Duncan it was a slower burning anger, a sulking that lasted and lasted and gave him the name Duncan *dubh*, Duncan the black, for his dark moods. They were different in other ways, too. Mary was as unmovable as a mountain when she had made up her mind to something, Duncan as changeable as the shadows on a Highland loch. He would start off up the hill to hunt for the fox's lair, then, when Mary had followed into the bracken or the berry thicket, he would change his mind and race off towards the stream to find a salmon. The only thing about Duncan that was steadfast was his desire to be where Mary was. He was a terrible boy for teasing and playing tricks, but when his tormenting turned Mary from him in anger or hurt, he would retreat into misery and, although it often seemed unfair, Mary would have to comfort him. But he took care of Mary in one important way. For there was something else about Mary that was not so of Duncan, or any of the other children in the glen. She had the *an dà shelladh*, the gift of the two sights. There were times she could see into the past, into the future, into the distance, and even into the hearts of others. People said Mary could see the wind.

She did not think it a gift. She hated it—the headaches, the rush of blackness, the frenzied need to warn those about whom she had the premonitions. She hated the strangeness of seeing a thing happen as though it were as real as the cotton grass on the hill, then having it happen exactly the same, days, weeks, or even years later. She hated being set apart in this way. Duncan hated it too. He did not tease her about the *an dà shelladh*, and because he didn't Mary felt he was her anchor, her protection from the glances and whispers of the other children, the hasty gestures some adults made to save themselves in case she put spells on them.

Once, in school, Annie Morrison had stumbled over her reading lesson and sworn to the dominie that "Mairi Urquhart has ill-wished me." Mr. Fraser had strapped Annie's hand until it was red and sore but she had tearfully stuck to her story and some of the children had talked afterwards about Mary being unchancy.

As a small child Mary had more than once begged her mother to take away the gift. "Gift! Gift!" she would storm, her eyes heavy with misery. "It is no gift. It is my misfortune."

"Mairi, Mairi, it is a sore thing, surely, but it is what you are and must be." Her mother's dark eyes would be sympathetic and she would give Mary a bit of honey on her oat bannock and rock her for comfort. Mary would not be comforted.

Old Mrs. Grant told her much the same thing. Mrs. Grant was the only person in the township who understood how Mary felt. She lived alone in her cottage under the brow of Drum Eildean across the burn, not far from the waterfall. Her husband was long since dead and her only son had gone to America before Mary was born. She too had the gift of second sight. It was to her the people of the glen went for spells against bad luck and ill wishes, and for the *taibhses*, the glimpses into the future she could sometimes give them. And although all the women in the glen were versed in herbal cures and knew the charms against ill, it was often felt that Mrs. Grant's gift and her healing hands gave the remedies special power.

The minister, Mr. Graeme, at St. Kilda's parish church, preached that it was sinful to believe in spells and the like and that those who did would burn for ever in hell. All the same, the people came to the spae wife for their needs, as people in the glen had always done.

Mary went often to the cottage where the rowan grew tallest, and the spicy-scented roses and the creamy-white yarrow grew thickest. She cared almost as much for this tall, stern, quiet old woman as she did for Duncan. And Mrs. Grant, who was so reserved with most people, talked to Mary of the pain of her own childhood as a seer, of her happy marriage, and of Donald, her son. She shared his letters from New England with Mary and told her that he was sending money so that she could go, some day, to live with him.

Over the years Mary learned the uses of the camomile, savoury, thyme, and lovage that grew in Mrs. Grant's garden and of the hawthorn, burdock, flag, gentian, and mint that grew wild on the hills and beside the streams, just by being with the old woman. She learned too some of the simple charms and spells for healing, the charms against ill-wishing and the evil eye, but when it came to studying seriously Mary refused, stubbornly. "I will not be set apart so," she would cry.

"Mairi, Mairi, you have the gifts. You have the *an dà shelladh*. You have the knowledge in your heart to turn away evil. You have the healing in your hands. And what gifts the good God gives us, those gifts must we cherish and nurture. Remember you well the story our own dear Lord tells of the talents.''

''I will not. Mother Grant, do not weigh me with such needs of folk. Is it not enough to have to see their ills before they do, themselves? Jenny Blackburn pained so in her back for the witch doll Mairi Carmichael set in the burn, sotted old Angus Morrison choking to death on his dram—what need have I of this?''

''What a body is given to do, a body must do— one way or another, Mairi.'' There was a tinge of sadness in Mrs. Grant's voice. She sighed and gave Mary an unaccustomed kiss on the top of her head.

Duncan would not go with Mary on those visits. He did not like her friendship with Mrs. Grant.

''Mairi,'' he had told her after her first long visit with the old woman. ''It was the royal stag himself I saw on Carroch Hill and I could have followed him but I would not without you.''

Mary had been bitterly disappointed. Then she had realized that there had been no deer, that it was only Duncan's way of telling her she was not to leave him. And every time she did there was a wondrous something Duncan had seen—a glimpse of the rare wildcat, a vixen that might have let them play with her kits, a shadow that was sure to have been the urisk over by the Corran Craig—that great shaggy grey half-man, half-goat everyone knew lived up by the rocky pool beyond the waterfall, though no one had ever seen it.

''Duncan *dubh*, you are not to mind so much.'' Contrite, Mary would not visit Mrs. Grant for a week or two.

All this Mary was remembering as she tramped around the meadow, whistling the lambs from the high crevices in the rocks where they loved to climb, checking now and then to see that the ewe and her new baby were all right. "Och, Duncan *dubh*, how could you have gone away at all!" she whispered furiously. "I would have hidden myself away in the *coire na cailleach* and never gone. Never. Never."

Ignoring the calls of the others as they herded their animals towards home, Mary stood on the slope of the pasture looking down over the hills. It had stopped raining. In that sudden brilliance of the sky that comes in unexpected moments in the Highlands, the pasture blazed with the gold of the whin and broom in flower, the honey-sweet perfume of them rich in the air. The little loch just below the slope was ringed with aspen and rowan and birch softly green with early leaf. Above its dark water, small black terns and the great curlews wheeled in uneven circles against the wind, the sharp keek-keek-keek of the terns punctuating the curlews' wild cries. High on Carroch Hill to the west, Donald Cameron's cows grazing on the ridge were silhouetted against the deep, gentian-blue sky. Far below, Loch Ness shone white as a white swan's wing and, away on the other side, the fields were green with spring. Beyond them the hills, smudged with the darkened purple of last autumn's heather, rose and fell and rose again like massive earthworks left by the giants who were once the sole inhabitants of the north country.

Mary loved the land fiercely. She felt as though she had been born out of its earth, that she was kin to the whin and broom and heather that grew so profusely over the hillsides, that there were tiny unseen roots growing along her body, reaching out for the land, drawing nourishment from it. Once she had told Duncan, "When I am old, I will lie myself down on the hill and my roots will push themselves into the earth and I will sleep. The grass will come to cover me then, and I will be part of the hill for ever."

"And I will be there, too!"

"You will, for we are not to be parted. And maybe, Duncan, there will be a rowan tree grow out of us and bring good fortune to all who dance around it."

For two thousand years and more, Mary's people had lived on this beautiful, harsh, unyielding soil. And, like all Highlanders, Mary knew where almost every one of her ancestors had lived, died, and been buried—and where and when their ghosts walked among the living. She knew too, as all her people did, where the ancient giants, gods, and heroes of the old religions walked, which were the places sacred to them and which belonged to the fairies.

The fairies, the *sitheachean*, once gods and heroes, the sole dwellers in the land, were now the kings and queens of the unseen world, emerging into this world to bring good luck to those they favoured, trouble to those they did not. People called them the good neighbours, the people of peace, hoping the flattering names would keep away the trouble. Some simply called them the old ones. Mary and Duncan called them that and,

11

because once they had been lost far from home and led to safety by a strange light, they had been sure that they were favoured and that one day they would find the old ones and perhaps meet a fairy cavalcade shining in the sun. They knew they would never fear the fairies.

But Duncan had gone away. At first the loneliness had seemed so unbearable that Mary had choked back her pride and asked Mrs. Grant for a charm to bring him home.

"It is not for this a seer has the healing gifts," Mrs. Grant had reproved her. And Mary had settled down, finally, to await Duncan's return. In time she had grown from a child to a young girl. Now, at fifteen, she was hardly taller than she had been at twelve and no more beautiful. But her hair was thick and long and shiny and she had a spark in her eyes and a quirk of humour that came and went from the corner of her wide mouth, and there was still an underlying sweetness to her nature that softened her sharp tongue and brought more than one boy, refusing to be afraid of her two sights, to come courting at her door. Astonished there would be any who imagined she would not wait for Duncan, she unceremoniously sent them all away.

Mary looked across the Great Glen through sudden tears. "I cannot come where you are, Duncan," she cried. The wind tore the words from her lips and carried them down into the valley but Duncan's voice in Mary's head, "Come, Mairi," in such pain, was still strong. Abruptly she gathered up her skirt, clutched her plaid at her neck, and headed up the slope.

With the rose and green check of the shawl making a bright sail behind her, her hair rippling in black waves above it, she ran across the fields, her bare feet scarcely touching the ground. She scrambled over the low stone dikes, leapt across the rushing streams, and at last clambered up the side of the high, round hill that overlooked the waterfall where the kelpie, the water horse, was said to rule.

All her life, in times of joy or trouble, Mary had come to this hill—the *tornashee*, the fairies' hill. Below it, near the burn, was the rowan tree where the children came to dance on May Morning, to tell their wishes and receive their luck. On the slopes of the hill the magic pearlwort, the safeguard against evil spells, and the velvet heart's-ease grew in greatest abundance. It was on that round summit that Mary and Duncan had been sure they would find the old ones one day.

She threw herself down on the hilltop, stretched out her arms, and put her ear against the ground. Sometimes, beyond the rustling noises of the grass and of the insects that burrowed beneath it, Mary could hear what might be the pipes and fiddles of fairy music, and once in a great while, in rare moments, she was sure she could hear the voice of the hill itself. It was a singing sound, a low, even, soft, thrumming, humming sound, sometimes joyful, sometimes sad, and it came from deep in the heart of the hill. In that sound joy and sorrow met and from it Mary often felt that she drew all her strength.

On this evening she was too upset to hear anything but the distress in her own heart. "I cannot go to Canada, och, how can I go?'' she whispered over and over. A sob was in her throat. "How can you ask it of me? Are you so unhappy? Why do you not come home? Duncan, I cannot.'' Even as she said the words, the frenzy was growing in her. How could she not go to him? She sat up, her hands clenched into tight fists. She knew she had no choice. She had to go to Canada—and as she thought it, the means of going came to mind.

She stumbled down the hill and across the few feet to where the old rowan tree stood. She put her face against it, her arms tightly around it. "Take my wishes,'' she whispered brokenly, "and bring me good fortune.'' Then she turned and walked stiffly back the way she had come.

CHAPTER II
The Cairngorm Brooch

It was already evening, way past milking time, when she reached the pasture. The little black cow was bawling. In a few swift movements, Mary untied the rope that had tethered it to a broom bush, yanking it impatiently. She made a cursory inspection of the ewe and its lamb and gave a sharp whoo-ee to the rest of the sheep and the goats, neglecting her usual words of affection and encouragement. She all but ran along the path to where the Urquhart cottage lay snuggled into a hollow of Carroch Hill. Moo-ing and maa-ing and baa-ing indignantly, bumping into each other along the way, the animals trotted after her.

With that same speed and impatience, Mary settled the disgruntled beasts in the byre, milked the cow, and carried the wooden pail to the low, hollowed stone by the cottage door. Hastily she murmured the words of greeting to the *bodach*, the house fairy whose presence brought good fortune to the family. She poured his milk into the stone for him, nervously smoothed the rough blue linen of her skirt, adjusted her shawl around her shoulders, took a deep breath, and went inside.

The cottage was small and its single room was dark and thick with the peat smoke that rose from the round hearth in its centre towards the chimney in the low roof. Mingling with the smoke were the odours of the boiled oats and kale keeping warm in the large iron pot that hung over the fire, and the cheese dripping from its cloth into the sink near the room's single window.

Mary always felt half smothered by the dark closeness of the cottage but, on this evening, she was too perturbed to notice.

"*Slan leat*," she greeted her mother, her father, and her sister Jeannie, as though she were not bothered in any way, and sat down at her place at the board table.

"Did Sally have her lamb, then?" Mary's mother rose from her place and dished kale and oatmeal porridge onto a wooden plate and poured a cup of buttermilk.

"She did that. A fine bit of a ewe lamb." Mary bowed her head, said her grace, and tried to eat. The talk was of the day's ploughing and spinning, of whether or not Patrick Grant was going to be able to manage his rent, of Jeannie's coming marriage to Johnny Fraser, but Mary did not listen. It was such a great thing, such a terrible thing she was going to ask. Suddenly she set her spoon on the table with a bang.

"I will be needing the cairngorm brooch." She almost shouted, she was so nervous. Someone—Jeannie or Mary's mother—gasped. Quietly, his face showing no emotion, her father said, "Mairi, I believe you spoke but I did not quite make out what it was you said."

Mary clenched her hands at her sides. Her pale face flushed but she spoke as evenly as her father. "I said, Father, that I will be needing the cairngorm brooch, it that lies wrapped in its linen in the kist." She nodded towards the large wooden chest that stood in the far corner of the room. Again there was the sound, softer this time, of sharply indrawn breath.

The brooch was a large, flat silver circlet, marked in an ancient Celtic pattern, the cairngorm stone in its centre the clear, peaty-brown colour of a Highland stream. The brooch had been given to a James Urquhart three hundred years earlier, after the battle of Flodden Field, because he had saved the life of his chief. It was handsome and the only possession of real value the Urquharts had.

Her father's usually ruddy face was white against his fire-red hair. His words dropped slowly, one by one, into the silent room.

"And what might you think you will be needing the brooch for?"

"It is for passage money."

"Och, Mairi, what is this?" cried her mother.

"It is to fetch Duncan away home."

"Mairi, you cannot—"

17

"Let the lass speak." James Urquhart had not taken his eyes from Mary's face.

"He promised he would come and he did not." Mary's low voice rose with every impassioned word she spoke as she told about hearing Duncan's voice. "And I could feel the pain of his pain and the need of his need and what is there in all the world but the brooch itself that will buy passage for me?"

In the silence that followed Mary did not, could not look at anybody. She was remembering a time four years back. At eleven, she had been old enough to go to work as a kitchen maid for Mr. and Mrs. Gillespie at the big house. Old enough to learn something of household skills, her mother had said. Mary had known the rudiments of cooking and spinning. She had always known how to wash clothes but never anything of weaving or knitting, the skills Jeannie had learned so well. And she had had no intention of learning them.

"It is not for me to be spending my life as a kitchen maid," she had told them. "I am meant for the beasts of the pasture."

"You will need to learn a thing or two more than caring for the cows and the sheep, my lass," her father had said. "And what is more, we will be needing the money your service will fetch."

Argument had been useless. The terms had been drawn up between James and Margaret Urquhart and the Gillespies at Tigh na shuidh and Mary had gone off over the hills and across the river with her change of shift, her Sunday-best skirt, and a precious pair of new leather brogans for her feet tied up in a square of fresh linen. Her hair was combed neatly down her back and she had a set look in her eyes that matched the stubbornness in her heart.

At Tigh na shuidh she had learned the ways of ladies and gentlemen, the workings of a big house, how to scrub fine silver and good pewter and china dishes, and a great deal more English than the dominie at the school at Balnacairn had taught. "Very promising," Mrs. Gillespie had said, but at the end of six months Mary had tied her spare shift, her Sunday-best skirt, and her brogans into her linen kerchief and gone back across the river and over the hills.

Greeting her father on her own doorstep, she had said, "It is not for me to be spending my life as a kitchen maid. I am meant for the beasts of the pasture." The money had had to be given back to Mr. and Mrs. Gillespie and Mary had gone back out into the hills to herd cows and sheep with Duncan. Six months later Duncan left the Glen.

Some memory of that time may have been in Mary's father's mind too. He stood up slowly and leaned, palms down, on the table. His grey eyes were almost black with anger, his hair had fallen over his forehead.

"The brooch has stayed in our family these three hundred years." He turned from the table and left the house.

Mary's mother said nothing. The set of her head under her white cap, the clatter of the wooden platters as she cleared the table, showed how upset she was. Jeannie reached over and put her hand on Mary's. Jeannie had red hair like her father, but her features were soft and her nature gentle. "Canada is a far place to go alone. Such a far place. It might be you would get there, Mairi, but you might not get home again.''

"That could not be did I have the passage money.''

"Passage money!'' Mary's mother spun around from the sink where she had been scouring the plates. "Passage money!'' Her black eyes—so like Mary's—were blazing. "You would take yourself by yourself thousands of miles after a voice in your head, and him not sending you thought or word these four years? Though he is my own nephew, son to my own brother, I say it, Duncan Cameron is a thoughtless and a sulky lad. Do Davie's or Jean's letters say that were it not for Duncan's willing hands they would be lost? They do not! They write of Callum's willing hands, of Callum's back-breaking work, and him but ten years old. Mairi, put him from you. You who are so strong-minded, so wilful about everything else, would follow that lad's restless piping wherever, whenever he cares to lead you. Do not you give your life away to him. There's better lads than he here in the glen. There's Callum Grant pining for but a smile from you, and others too. Do not think of this again.''

"Mother!'' It was so unlike her mother to speak out violently in any cause. Mary was shocked, then swiftly angered. "Mother, I will not listen. Duncan and I....'' Mary clamped her mouth shut, and with the same stiff back her father had shown, she left the house.

She started straight up the slope in the direction of the *tornashee*. She had not gone far before her steps began to slow and finally halted.

"They are right. How dared I ask for that? How could I have?" Her face grew hot from shame. "What am I to do?" She sat down, her head in her hands. She was shaking from shame, from the sting of her mother's words and her father's anger. She longed to go ask for the comfort of forgiveness—but could not. She needed to go where Duncan called—but could not do that either. Tormented, she began to pace up and down the slope. "Mother, Father, Jeannie!" she cried, begging for their help.

But there was no help for her.

"I must find Duncan. I must. He is in such need." She started back down the slope towards the path. "I cannot go home now. I cannot face them. Somehow I must go!" On the path she stopped once more. The last of the day was gone. The evening mist had lifted and the moon shone bright over the land. From where she stood Mary could just see the heather thatch of her home. She brushed the tears from her eyes and took a deep, shaky breath. She dropped to her knees and whispered a prayer for her mother, her father, her sister, the animals, the house, and, finally, "all who may come to stay in it while I am gone." For the length of a single heartbeat she hesitated, then turned away and continued resolutely down the hill towards the road leading to the west.

With the first step the old Gaelic mourning words began inside her, "*och-on, och-on,*" and as she went she could hear them echoing from the rushing water of the burns and in the wind along the hills, "*och-on, och-on, och-on,*" alas, alas, alas.

CHAPTER III

The *Andrew MacBride*

"Are you leaving, then, Mairi, without a word of farewell?"

Mary stopped.

"Will you leave without the breath of one small word?"

Mary spun around. It was Mrs. Grant, her tall frame and the white of her bonnet clearly outlined in the moonlight. A sad but affectionate look crossed her strong, old face. She held Mary with her steady gaze for a long minute, then she spoke in low, measured tones.

"You will make your voyage but it will bring you sorrow and many trials. Twice will you refuse your destiny, twice will you seek it before you embrace it as your own." She paused. "The dark holds grave danger for you, Mairi. Beware the dark."

An owl hooted near the small loch just below the path. The scent of the whin flowers was strong on the night air. Mary's heart was racing and it was a moment or two before she could reply.

"Would it be better that I not go?" she whispered, at last.

"What will be will be," answered the old woman. "I have three gifts to travel with you. One is for need. One is for good fortune. One is for blessing." She pressed a paper packet into one of Mary's hands, a spindle whorl into the other. She laid a fine, soft wool plaid of red and black and green tartan over Mary's arm. Then she bent down and kissed her gravely on both cheeks, turned, and strode away up the path.

Mary stood for a long time as though rooted to the ground. She looked at Loch Ness glimmering in the moonlight far below. She looked up the path at Mrs. Grant retreating into the distance. Three times she started after her, three times she hesitated, and at last turned her steps downward.

She marched purposefully down the long hill and along the shore of Loch Ness for almost half the night, trying desperately not to think about Mrs. Grant, her mother, her father, or Jeannie, hearing only Duncan's "Come, Mairi," and over and over the mourning words, *och-on, och-on*, as though she never meant to return.

When she came to the ruins of Urquhart Castle she stopped, exhausted. She sheltered under a low, crumbling stone wall against the cold of the heavy mist and the pre-dawn wind, sleeping fitfully, wrapped in her rough plaid until it was light enough to see what was in the packet Mrs. Grant had given her.

The packet held two English five-pound notes. With the money there was a letter.

> *Mo Mairi, gràdach*
>
> Here is money for your passage. I who am aged, I who have lived on Drum Eildean all my life, will not leave it. I who was married in the plaid I give you do not wish to be buried in it. It is for you to be married in and my blessing comes with it. The spindle whorl is very old. My great-grandmother told me she had it from her great-grandmother and that it was already old when she used it. It is made from rowan wood for your good fortune. May our Lord and all his angels travel with you.
>
> Elizabeth Grant

Mary looked at the money in her lap, the money Donald Grant had been sending his mother from America for thirty years. It was so much! She stroked the worn wood of the spindle whorl. How like Mrs. Grant to give her this double amulet—a rowan wood spindle—against evil spells. She got up from the shadow of the cold, damp wall. She paced around the ruins, now putting her hands on the mossy stones, now looking up at the grey sky from the grass- and weed-covered floor of the roofless castle hall. For one surprised moment she saw the stone floor and a black-beamed ceiling and a fire on a great hearth. A woman in a green gown stood before the fire.

"Greetings, lady," Mary murmured politely, not wanting to be ill-wished by the *glaistig* who haunted the home of her family's long-ago chiefs. She was used to these unexpected glimpses into the other world. She went outside and climbed down the cliff to the water's edge.

She looked down at her small, white face reflected in the lake water, her hair hanging down on either side like two broad, black silk ribbons. She tried a friendly smile but only one corner of the reflection's mouth turned up ruefully. She put her hand down and churned up her watery likeness.

"I cannot take the money," she told herself unhappily, although the words "Mary, my dear one" touched her almost unbearably. "It is well and good for her to say she will not go from Drum Eildean but there is Donald." She looked at, but did not really see, a pair of moorhens gathering twigs close by the shore. The money was more than enough, she was sure, to buy her passage and provisions to take her to Upper Canada. But the realization that Upper Canada was three thousand miles away was beginning to sink into her awareness. She knew the journey took seven weeks when the weather was clear and the seas calm. And she had heard tales of ships that foundered at sea in the great Atlantic storms. She was going into this danger and she had spoken not a word of farewell to her family. "I cannot go!" she said aloud. The moorhens bobbed nervously off from shore.

Even as she spoke, she was beset by dizziness and Duncan's face came to her, not as she remembered it but older-looking, as he must be now, with such desperation in his eyes that she sprang to her feet, stuffed the money and the spindle whorl into the pocket of her skirt, tucked Mrs. Grant's beautiful old shawl under her arm, and scrambled back up to higher ground and the path that led to the west.

It was forty miles to the port town of Fort William but it seemed like forty thousand to Mary. Sometimes sick with headache and apprehension she ran, jogged, stumbled along the path, hardly noticing the brambles that caught at her clothes and scratched her arms, legs, and face, hardly feeling the sharp stones and twigs under her bare feet. Sometimes she slowed to a brisk stride, intensely aware of the mountains looming over her, the flowers blooming along the way, and the birds singing in every tree.

"I will come back again. I will," she cried, causing a group of travellers to quicken their steps as they passed and to scarcely nod in greeting.

She stopped for the night—during a heavy rain—to eat and sleep in a house. It was near where she crossed the River Oich, a mile or so past Fort Augustus. She frightened the kindly old couple who gave her supper and a bed by her scratched and dishevelled appearance and the distraught look in her eyes. She knew it and could do nothing about it.

Sometimes her natural good humour asserted itself. She sang with the birds in the early morning as she bathed in the river. Once she stopped to get a drink of water from a small boy at a spring. She shared their noon meal with a gang of men working on the canal that was to connect the chain of lochs along the Great Glen.

The mountains were growing higher as she neared Fort William. Late in the afternoon of the second day Ben Nevis came in sight, towering over the whole mountain range, higher than any mountain Mary had ever seen. But its great, rounded bulk, covered with snow, looked for all the world like the white wool on the back of a fat old ewe. Mary smiled.

She reached the edge of town by evening. "Here is it, then," she told herself bravely. "Well, it is not so grand, even, as is Inverness." She smoothed her hair as best she could and straightened her skirt.

The town was one long street running parallel to Loch Linnhe, the big sea loch that harboured the sailing ships from the west. Short, busy, narrow streets led from the high street to the piers and warehouses crowded with people shouting and calling over the screech of the big white gulls along the water's edge. The fort that gave the town its name stood guard over the northern end of it, the red-coated soldiers visible against the grey stone walls.

Refusing to be intimidated, Mary marched into town. She enquired of an old woman selling eggs where she might find a sailing ship, and the old woman directed her to the ship owners' offices. Mary found passage on the *Andrew MacBride*, sailing within the week.

Next she found herself lodging, at a terrible amount of money, in a dingy little room with a lumpy bed she had to share not only with bugs but with three other women. They were the Macfeeters from Invergarry, they told her, a mother and two daughters, all sailing on the *Andrew MacBride*.

Mary did not like them, their dirty, unkempt hair and clothes, or their never-ceasing talk of the soldiers at the fort and the fancy clothes they meant to buy.

The following morning she found the market and bought her provisions for the voyage: oats for bannock, potatoes, cheese, and a few dried apples. Emboldened by the success of her venture, she bought a change of clothing too: a linen shift and skirt, a pair of woollen stockings, a pair of brogans, and a comb. She was pleased with herself for having managed so well, although it seemed to her that the linen was not as finely woven nor the dye so rich a blue as that at home. The shoes were poorly made and the whole cost a great deal more than she had thought it would. She bought a basket for the food and made bundles of the clothes and lugged them to her lodging.

Flora Macfeeter was in the room changing her clothes. For an instant Mary saw an image of Flora, old, tired, and sour-looking, but she said nothing to the smiling face. Flora told Mary where she might buy a sheet of paper to write a letter home. "And we will look after your things," she said kindly. "It will be my mother or it will be Margaret or me will be here. Och, if it were my back—on this warm day I could not bear the weight of a *single* plaid."

But Mary was not comfortable without her old shawl and nothing in heaven or earth could have convinced her to let go of one of Mrs. Grant's gifts for a single moment.

She found the stationer's shop and wrote her letter. "Please forgive me," she wrote, "for I cannot help myself. You know I must go.'' She signed it, ''Your loving Mairi,'' and left a blot by her name where a tear had fallen. By good fortune the stationer had a relative on his way to Invermoriston whose brother was courting a girl in Inchnatarf and would carry the letter up the glen.

Mary was so relieved at how well matters were turning out that she wasn't in the least upset to discover, on her way back to her lodging, a bill posted to say that the *Andrew MacBride*'s sailing was delayed for three days. Cheerfully she hurried to tell the Macfeeters the news.

When she got there, the room was empty. No Macfeeters. No luggage—not theirs, not hers. Frantically Mary peered into all the corners. On her hands and knees she searched under the bed. There was nothing anywhere. She stood up. For one shocked moment she stared at the empty room. Then she began to curse. ''May all the devils in Scotland be after them! May they be hapless and wan, loveless and glum, shrivelled and sour. May dearth southward, dearth northward, dearth eastward and westward be always with them, those spawn of the speckled devil!'' She burst into tears.

Suddenly, in the midst of a sob, she remembered that she still had both Mrs. Grant's fine wool plaid and her own rough one. She was so relieved that she stopped crying at once. She rubbed her tears away and sat on the bed to count her money— enough to buy sparse provisions for a seven-week voyage. Nothing for a skirt or shift.

''I shall reach Canada with naught but the clothes on my back—and those in rags,'' she wailed. ''Och, why is it that I who see so much I do not want to see cannot see my own bad fortune on its way?" She remembered the image of Flora Macfeeter's face, old and sour, and was glad. She looked at the few coins in her hands. She looked at her feet. "And I have brogans that pain me." She choked back a fresh sob, reached down, and yanked off the shoes. She stood up, hung them around her neck by their laces, grabbed both her shawls, and stomped down the stairs muttering, "I will find those thieving women."

Up and down the crowded little streets of Fort William Mary tramped. It was, as Flora Macfeeter had said, very warm. In and out of shops and taverns she went, her face white and set, her back stiff, ignoring the rude invitations of men in taverns and the persistent shoves and shouts of pedlars in the streets. The three Macfeeters (if indeed that was their name, Mary thought venomously) were not to be found.

It was well past the dinner hour by the time she had peered fruitlessly and nervously into the last tavern, and she was hungry, thirsty, tired, and dispirited. She reached into her pocket to reassure herself that her money was still there. "But I cannot spend it on dinner," she realized with sinking heart, "or I will starve on the ship. But how will I even last the days to the sailing if I starve now?" Wearily she trudged down to the waterfront and sat at the end of the pier from which, in three days' time, a rowboat would take her to where the *Andrew Mac-Bride* lay at anchor. Through the haze a large white gull appeared, diving for a fish.

Mary closed her eyes and put her tired feet in the water. Behind her, people were walking along the front. Dimly she heard them chatting and calling to each other in a dozen different accents—sometimes in English, more often in Gaelic, now and then in some unintelligible foreign tongue. Two passed by whose accents were from her own glen and she was assailed by such a wave of homesickness that she cried aloud.

Several people stopped to make sure she was not ill and a kind face leaned over her. "Such a wee lass all alone." The woman put her hand on Mary's shoulder. Mary sprang to her feet and hurried from the pier. She did not want to answer anybody's questions about anything. She marched smartly through the town as though bent on some errand, though actually not paying attention to where she was going, until she found herself on the road that led, eventually, back to her own glen.

When she realized where she was headed her step lightened. She kept right on going. By evening she had reached the village of Spean Bridge. She stopped for a meal and a night's lodging with a large family. Happily she gathered the smaller children around her and told them stories of wicked people in bad towns. When she noticed their mother casting envious glances at the shoes she still had strung around her neck, she gave them to her.

"It was foolishness to buy them." She smiled. "I do not need them now." But in the night she dreamed of Duncan's large, dark, beseeching eyes and his sad voice calling and calling. In the morning his face was still before her, his eyes still pleading. Now, with her own eyes open or shut, she could see him, hear him. She knew she could not go home no matter how she longed to; for Duncan's sake, for Mrs. Grant's sake—there was all Donald's money.

"Mairi! Mairi! There is not the road to the north," the children shouted after her as she started off.

"I am going back to the town to wait for a ship that will be soon sailing," she called to them.

"But those wicked people will get you."

"Do you give me your blessing, then?"

"We do, we do," they shouted.

"Then I will fare well." Mary returned to Fort William in better spirits.

With greater care and more canny bargaining than the first time, Mary bought food for the voyage—what a meagre amount it seemed! Mistrustful and without money, she could not look for lodging, and she would not stay in the old warehouses where she had seen that others had put themselves up. She slung the sacks of oats and potatoes over her back and tramped out to the hills, to Ben Nevis. A little way up its great flank she found a deep corrie. There she hid her sacks on a ledge and sheltered herself from the rain and the dark. She was very hungry. But she dared not eat any of the food she had bought. Instead she foraged for what was left of last season's nuts, seeds, and berries, and for the young, green ferns and cresses growing along the edges of the streams. For the first time in her life she was glad of the knowledge she had from Mrs. Grant about which plants were edible and which were poisonous.

Every morning she walked the four and a half miles into town to make sure the *Andrew MacBride* was not sailing without her, then she trudged back to her cave. Once she asked for a bit of oat bannock from the weaver who lived at the edge of town, but when he demanded a kiss in return she told him he might grow toads in his beard if he were not more careful where he asked his kisses. Swiftly he crossed himself and threw the bannock after her. She would not give him the satisfaction of seeing her pick it up; she left it lying where it fell.

Only once did she dip into her supply—greedily she ate a handful of oats. The rest of the time her will power held and she subsisted on the wild plants. "Och, Duncan *dubh*," she said ruefully on a day when there was only one small fern to be found, "it may be I will starve, then all you will have for your comfort will be the shade of me."

Sometimes her headache was so intense and her need to reach Duncan so great she was sure she would explode and could not even think of eating.

The ship sailed at last on an evening when the tide was high. It was the first clear night since Mary had returned to Fort William and the dark outline of Ben Nevis stood out against the stars as the ship moved out of the harbour. A piper who was going to the new land played "This Is My Departing Time" for those who were leaving their homeland for ever. They lined the ship's railing, holding each other for comfort, weeping.

Mary felt only relief that her ocean journey was beginning at last. "Soon, Duncan, I will be with you soon," she whispered as she watched the big, round mountain disappear from sight.

CHAPTER IV
The Dark Forest

Quarters in the hold of the *Andrew MacBride* were a nightmare. Mary's berth was the top one of three, set in a row only two feet from other rows, in a space no crofter would stall three dozen cows and sheep in. It was to house two hundred people. What air there was was soon dark and fetid with the odours of the two hundred unwashed bodies, their breath, their excrement, and their cooking. It was dark and it was cold—cold for being so airless, as the Highland wind and rain had never been cold.

Out on deck the sea terrified her. It rose to the heights of the highest hills, it fell to the depths of the deepest glens, in a constant motion that seemed to threaten, with each new swell, to engulf the ship that rode it so precariously.

Although she was violently sick to her stomach

from the pitching and rolling, Mary was so glad the voyage had actually begun that, almost, she did not mind. In the bunks below hers were Kirsty and Iain Mackay, their new baby, and Kirsty's mother, Elizabeth Finlay. When she first met her Mary saw the grey mist of death around Kirsty's pale hair but she could not bear to say so. The family were so good to her, so genuinely eager to share their provisions, that soon she was cooking her porridge and potatoes with them, helping to care for the baby and commiserating with them over their sorrows.

They had come from a glen to the north and west of Mary's, they told her one evening after supper. "And had our houses burned out behind us so we could not go home"—there were tears in Kirsty's blue eyes, there was bewilderment in her soft voice as well as bitterness—"so our chiefs could have our land for the sheep. Our own chiefs whose fathers were our fathers, whose mothers were our mothers."

Iain said nothing, but the set of his red head bent over the rattle he was whittling for the baby bespoke not only bitterness but resignation.

"It is a new land we go to." Elizabeth's bonnet strings bobbed with her firm nod. "A good land, we will be well there." Elizabeth's husband was already in Upper Canada awaiting them.

"A good land." They were the words Uncle Davie had written. It was what he had said when he had first talked of leaving the glen. Thoughts of leaving the Highlands had been in the air for three generations, to be sniffed out of corners and tasted on the wind. They had begun after the Scottish followers of Prince Charles Edward Stuart, the Bonnie

Prince, had lost to the English at the bloody battle
of Culloden Moor, sixty-nine years earlier, in 1746.
Many of the Highland men who had survived the
battle had been exiled. Later, others had chosen to
leave with their families. The settlers in America
and the Canadas had written home to say that it was
fine to have no landlords. Shipping companies had
posted bills in all the market towns saying that land
across the sea could be had for only a few shillings.
Preachers, influenced by wealthy landowners or
honestly feeling it would be better for the people,
preached that it was a gift from God. Mr. Graeme at
St. Kilda's told his congregation, "He has given you
a chance to repent you of your sins and begin life
anew." And Uncle Davie Cameron had sat afterwards by the Urquhart hearth and called emigra-
tion wisdom.

"Wisdom is it, Davie Cameron?" James Urquhart
had raised one red eyebrow scornfully. "We have
been in this glen from time immemorial, Urquharts
and Camerons alike." But Uncle Davie had sold up
and gone with Aunt Jean and Duncan and Callum
and wee Iain. The family had settled in the backwoods of Lake Ontario country, among refugees
from the revolution in America.

Uncle Davie had written again and again to beg
James and Margaret to join him in Upper Canada.
War had broken out anew in 1812 between the
British colonies in Canada and the thirteen old colonies, now called the United States, but "we are not
much troubled here on our island at our end of the
loch," he had said and had drawn them a map to
show how to find him. Mary had pored over it,

learning it by heart, trying in her mind to fill it with hills and streams and crofts, trying to see Duncan's dark forests, aching to see him in his new world. But the second sight did not come to her at will, it came and went unbidden. Duncan and his dark forest had remained stubbornly beyond her view.

"And here am I, now," she thought, looking around her at the sorry gathering of exiles, "with these poor souls who have no homes left to go back to."

The exiles did their best to be cheerful. Hector Macmillan, the piper, played dance tunes and melodies they all knew how to sing, and there were story-tellers. But the sailors sometimes played cruel jokes on the passengers in the hold and stole their provisions—the Mackay family lost their dried berries, their bit of salt fish, and a bag of oats. After four weeks the drinking water was stale and scarce and a lot of the food had spoiled. Many people had sickened of dysentery and malnutrition. Peggy Gordon grew hysterical from homesickness, Jamie Mathieson swore he would jump overboard before he would pick one more rat from his oats. Kirsty Mackay weakened day by day from the poor food and, one stormy night, she died in her sleep. Her thin body was rolled in her plaid and Colin Macleod, who had been the dominie back in Kirsty's glen, read psalms from the Bible, and her body was cast into the sea.

For one horrible instant, as Mary watched the plaid sink, she felt an almost overpowering urge to jump after it. It was as though she were the one sinking and had to leap in to save herself. Forcing back the sensation of black, suffocating water, she clung to the ship's rail until her knuckles went white and her breath came in sharp gasps. Afterwards she wept until there were no more tears in her. She crouched on the deck and wearily rested her head against the railing, her hair whipping about her in wet swirls. The frenzy that had been driving her for so long had abated, the headache was gone. In their place she was filled with a sadness that drained her of all other feeling.

She did not want to sleep again in the hold. She ate her oats raw, on deck; she wrapped herself in her plaid and tried to sleep with her head on her sack, braving the waves that passed over her, the winds that threatened to hurl her overboard. But the waves were too powerful and in the end the wind caused her to flee in terror to her berth below. Hugging herself, saying charms over and over, she kept the fears at bay.

The day after Kirsty Mackay died, when the emigrants had come together on deck around the piper, Mary took the baby from its grieving father and stood at the edge of the gathering. After the piper had played "The Flowers of the Forest" she sang a lullaby for the baby and for Kirsty. All the days afterwards she took the baby to walk with her around and around the deck.

Three weeks later the ship sailed into the gulf of the St. Lawrence and began its journey up the great river towards Montreal. At first the fog was too thick for anyone to be able to see anything. When it finally lifted Mary could not believe they were on a river, it was so wide. As the days passed it gradually narrowed and the shores became visible, faintly at first, then more and more clearly—low and rolling to the south, high and rising towards the Laurentian Mountains away to the north.

Along both shores were farms and villages with neat little white houses and tall shiny church spires. The distant mountains brought a joy to Mary's heart. "The forests are so far from where the people must be," she thought. "Why do you mind them so, Duncan? Are the hills so different from our own?"

Slowly they made their way up the river, past settled islands, the mouths of smaller rivers, and more and more villages—everywhere the signs of settled countryside. High on its promontory, the city of Quebec guarded the river. Mary thought that, but for there being no castle, it must be as fine, even, as Edinburgh itself—the fort, the stone houses both down along the shore and up above the cliff.

They finally docked in Montreal on a morning in mid-July. The day was already hot and damp and the air was full of bugs. The quay gave off an odour of dead fish, of cargoes and people emerging from ships from all over the world. Mary felt overwhelmed by the noise of hundreds of people all shrieking and shouting at each other in different languages. It was not what she had expected of a city in Duncan's "dark forest".

She determined not to stay in this hot, stinking, crowded place a single moment. She would have struck out for the spot on Uncle Davie's map called Collivers' Corners in Upper Canada with no delay but Elizabeth Finlay invited her to travel with her party. Elizabeth Finlay and Iain Mackay, and a few others who were headed west, were travelling on that day by coach. "And there's room for you," Elizabeth told Mary, "room going begging." Carefully not looking at Mary's bare feet, her now faded and threadbare blue skirt and worn blouse, she insisted, "Mairi, in these long, sad weeks, you have become very dear to us—to Iain and to me and to the wee bairnie. Why do you not come with us all the way?"

Mary, looking from Elizabeth's kind, worn face to Iain's weary one, read in their eyes—without the need of second sight—the hope that she would marry Iain and be mother to the baby.

"I will come with you, and many thanks, as far as Cornwall on the river, but I must go on to Loch Ontario."

They did not have to stay the night in Montreal since the stage-coach in which Iain had booked passage left immediately for Upper Canada. It wasn't long before the road grew narrow and the forests grew thick. There was little light. Mary began to understand why Duncan had written "dark with forest". In some places the trees were the familiar birch and aspen. In other places all she could see was cedar and tamarack swamp. But along most of the route were giant pines rising a hundred feet and more into the air, their trunks over six feet across, their branches starting only thirty or forty feet from the ground and meeting high above the rough road. Before the coach had driven very far into the forest Mary had to restrain herself from pushing open the door, jumping out, and running back to the river, back to the city, to where those gigantic trees would not close in on her so relentlessly. Firmly she said to herself a charm against danger.

> I will close my fist
> Tight I will close my fist
> Against the danger
> That I have come within.

With each passing mile from Montreal, the smaller, rougher, and farther apart were the settlements—squares and notches cut out of the wilderness. Many of them were only one or two rude shacks, with blankets for doors, surrounded by a few feet of raw tree stumps with the cut-down trees in high piles at the edge of the clearing. "Bush country," a fellow traveller called the woods they rode through. His voice was loud and nasal and his English flat and harsh to Mary's ears used to the soft sibilant sounds of Gaelic.

The coach lurched and bumped along the deeply rutted road, now and again all but capsizing on a protruding root, a stump, or a larger boulder. Occasionally there was relief from the endless trees when the road ran alongside the St. Lawrence River, past rapids or through more settled villages where there were a few stone or frame houses with flowers and vegetables growing around them. The journey took two days with two overnight stops at dirty little inns that stood at crossroads along the way.

At last they reached Cornwall, a sizeable town on the river with several inns, mills, and blacksmith shops. There Mary parted from her friends, they to travel north, she to follow the map she had memorized so carefully.

"I know it is many miles yet to Loch Ontario and farther still to the island where Uncle Davie lives but I will be well." She drew the map for them on the back of the paper packet that still held Mrs. Grant's letter and they asked the innkeeper about the distance. "Yep," he said, "looks to be up past Kingston way—be about a hundred miles."

"Mairi, you will get lost in this strange place. You are unprotected. Come with us for now and we will get word to your uncle. He will surely come for you."

"I cannot." Mary smiled. She took Elizabeth's hand. "I will not be lost. I have my map. The sound of the river will be always beside me. And—and I have money. I will be well." Mary hugged them all. "Fare you well." She kissed the baby once more. "Remember me."

But she did not have money and, alone, she did not feel as brave or cheerful as she let on. She, who had never been afraid of much of anything in either the seen or the unseen world, was afraid of this strange land, of strange people—Indians, about whom she had heard so many frightening stories, and others who spoke English so loudly in such flat accents; and even more, so much more, she was afraid of the forest that seemed to come at her from a depth of darkness too black to fathom, too powerful to escape.

Humming "The Battle Song of Harlaw" to keep up her courage, she set out with a will and walked steadily until nightfall. The road was very rough even on feet toughened by fifteen years of treading on rocks and sharp, cropped Highland grass. Her two shawls began to seem a real burden. There was no wind, the heat lay heavy and damp and thick, and the bugs were an unbelievable torment. In the Highlands the black clouds of whining, itching mosquitoes were unknown. Overhead where the trees almost met there were crows and jays and waxwings, birds she knew, and enormous pigeons of a kind she did not. They seemed to her friendly and, with their coo-roo-coo-roo, a bit of comfort in this strange place.

She passed half a dozen homesteads and several travellers on horseback, in carts, and once in a coach. She stopped at a log shack to ask for a cup of milk. A small, grey-looking man was sitting on a stump in the dooryard. "This ain't no inn and we don't feed beggars," he growled.

Before Mary could respond, a woman appeared from the interior of the cabin, equally grey-looking.

"Git along!" she spat. "Git along outta here."

Mary stared at her in horror.

"Scat," hissed the woman.

Mary left, dazed. She could never have imagined a human being talking to a stranger, a traveller, like that, "as though I were a dangerous beast," she muttered to herself.

Maybe because she was so shaken by the experience, maybe because she was bone-weary, Mary made a mistake. She had been running, walking, and running again along the ever-narrowing road for some time when she stopped. She was hungry and she was bitten from head to foot by mosquitoes, and while she had been running the tree-dim world had turned to night. She listened.

"I cannot hear the river." She was frozen with fright. She realized that it had been some time since she had seen either a dwelling or another traveller. She looked down and saw, by the bit of daylight that remained, that the road was no longer much more than a foot path. She began to hear the sounds of the woods at night as though she had just wakened from a sleep—wolves howling nearby, owls hooting, frogs croaking, other unfamiliar cries and calls, and all around her rustlings and gruntings in the underbrush.

"Duncan!" she whispered. "Duncan, I am lost." She hugged her two plaids as though they were her only comfort in the world.

Through the dark and the trees she saw a flicker of light. She ran towards it—off the path and into swamp water up to her hips. She screamed. She grabbed at a low branch of a cedar tree. She pulled herself up—and came face to face with a dark man looking down at her. She gasped, let the branch go, and would have fallen back into the swamp if the man hadn't grasped her by the arm and shoulder and pulled her back onto firm ground.

"Please," she pleaded in Gaelic, "please, let me go." She could not understand his reply. It was not English. She could see now that he was naked from the waist up. An Indian! A savage! She wrenched her arm free and ran. She fell, picked herself up, stumbled and ran again, gasping and sobbing, until she fell over a root.

She lay there, gulping in air, trying to calm herself, listening for the sound of feet coming after her. She could hear no feet. She heard the animals, she heard the owls—and then she heard the river.

"The river!" She sat up and looked around. She could make out nothing but the shape of evergreen trees.

"I do hear it," she whispered. "I will not leave this place until morning comes. Och, Duncan, what a terrible country this is. How will I find my way out of this wilderness? Is there no one to rescue me? My poor white bones will be found, years from this day, all picked over. My luck has surely left me." In a panic she felt into the pocket under her petticoat for the spindle whorl and for Mrs. Grant's letter. Safe. In spite of herself, she leaned against the trunk of a tree and dozed fitfully, like a cat, starting to wakefulness at every new sound.

At first light she saw that the wider road was only a few feet from where she sat. "What a foolish lass I am," she reproved herself. If she hadn't been so tired and so wet and dirty, she might have laughed. As it was, grimly she straightened her blouse and her skirt now stained with brown swamp water and pulled her fingers through her tangled hair. She picked up her shawls—Mrs. Grant's wrapped carefully inside her own—held her shoulders back, and started west along the road. She was too afraid of getting lost again to go down to the river to wash or drink.

Rescue did come and in an unexpected form. Mary hadn't been walking for more than half an hour when a coach rattled by. It stopped just up the road.

A woman's head in a fashionable bonnet poked out of the window. "Dear, dear," she fluttered, "what can you be doing on this desolate stretch of road at such an hour, child? It's only just gone seven."

Mary wanted to say, "What is it you think I am doing? I am making a fine meal of meat and drink on this white linen cloth you see spread out before your eyes." What she did say was, "I am on my way to Collivers' Corners, ma'am—on Loch Ontario."

"Why, that's a blessing. We're on our way to Amherst. That's on Lake Ontario."

"Mama, Josie's wet herself." A tousle-headed boy put his head out of the window beside his mother's.

"Just a minute, Charles, just a minute. Oh dear, oh dear! We've lost our nanny. It's so sad. Maggie died on board ship and I don't know what we shall do. I...you...we...you wouldn't be able to help with the children, would you? You do seem small." The woman looked doubtfully at Mary's ragged, grubby state. "They're very sweet," she added.

By this time the three children had crowded their mother out of the window and Mary could see, at once, that they were not sweet.

"I can see that they are," she agreed, "and I will be happy to help you care for them." Before the woman could change her mind, Mary hopped up onto the step and was in the coach.

The mother, an English woman named Sophie Babbington, had no rein on her children, and they, delighted to have a fresh victim, climbed all over Mary, shrieked in her ear, pummelled her viciously,

47

pulled her hair, and fought with each other across and on top of her. Mary didn't care. Mrs. Babbington had a wicker hamper full of cold chicken and white bread, and cold tea and fruit, food Mary had never eaten in her life, and the coach was steadily moving westward towards the dot on Uncle Davie's map that was labelled Collivers' Corners.

At Prescott, where the rapids ended, Mrs. Babbington, without a word, bought Mary a ticket on the ship that would take them up the river to Kingston on Lake Ontario and, from there, to Soames for Mary, and on to Amherst for herself and her children. She took a room in an inn at Prescott, saw to it that Mary had a bath, and gave her a skirt, a petticoat, a blouse, and a pair of shoes that had been the nanny's. Maggie had been only a little larger than Mary and the clothes did very well. They were clean but every bit as heavy as Mary's own in the heat. With a sigh, Mary bundled up her own rags to salvage as best she could another day. After a night's sleep in a real bed, even though none too clean and shared with all three children, she felt considerably brighter and well able to tackle the rest of her journey.

By the time their ship neared the island the children were Mary's devoted slaves. She had told them stories from Cornwall to Prescott, from Prescott to Kingston, from Kingston to Soames, each story more terrifying than the last. She had told them she was a witch and taught them nonsense rhymes in Gaelic that she said were evil spells. When the time came for her to leave them at Soames they all cried and Mrs. Babbington begged her to stay with them.

"I declare, the children have never behaved themselves so well. I don't know how you manage them!" Mrs. Babbington had slept in the coach from the moment she had picked Mary up, and as soon as they boarded the ship she had left the children completely to her.

Mary was as grateful to Mrs. Babbington and her children as they to her. They had kept her so busy she had had no chance to think of anything else. "*Beannachd Dhé leat*, may the blessing of God attend you," she said as she left them on the wharf at Soames. "I will not forget your kindness."

Soames was a prosperous village with five docks, short streets running from them to a main street where there were three inns, a couple of blacksmith shops, a livery stable and two mills. At one of the blacksmith shops Mary was told, "It ain't more'n eight miles to Collivers' Corners. Like as not you can get a lift if you wait."

She did not wait. Eight miles was nothing to walk. But the trees, once she had left the village, seemed taller and if possible even more formidable than the ones near Cornwall. And there was a steady wind here that moved the enormous treetops so that they seemed to be singing a constant, low, keening song. The road was much like the one out of Montreal and Cornwall. "Government road," the blacksmith had told her proudly, "wider than most. Goes all the way to the town of York, more than one hundred miles west of here."

As she tramped along in the half-light, Mary concentrated on the familiar sounds of pigeons and doves cooing. She started at the sight of strange animals and she tried not to acknowledge the terror that rose in her throat when she glanced into the dark trees hemming her in. She did not hear the horse and cart approach. She jumped and whirled around at the sound of a drawn-out "Whoa!"

"Didn't mean to scare you." The tall boy driving the cart looked concerned. "It ain't exactly that these here wagons is quiet or sneaky. Hop aboard if you like."

He was a tall, brown-haired boy perhaps three or four years older than she, with a broad, open face. Without a word she climbed up beside him.

"I'm Luke Anderson." He eyed her curiously. Mary told him her name and where she was headed. As she sat beside Luke, Mary's head reached only to his shoulder, and her feet did not quite touch the floor. She wished, for once, that she were not so small. With her feet dangling down like that she felt foolish. Once or twice Luke offered conversation but, when Mary did not respond, fell silent. He remarked about a bird in sudden flight and a deer that bounded across the road. Once they had to stop when a strange, ungainly, dark-furred animal lumbered across the road. "Raccoon," Luke replied to Mary's astonished question. Otherwise they rode for almost two hours in silence. The only sounds were the dull thud-thud of the horses hoofs on the dirt road and the chatter and whistle of the birds at the edge of the forest.

They came in sight of the village at last—a blacksmith shop, a general store, a scattering of log cabins and frame houses and, across a small stream, a dark red house beside a tall stone mill.

"That's the Corners," said the boy. Only then did Mary tell him, "I am wanting to find Davie Cameron and his family."

"Oh, that's too bad. That's really too bad. They took off from here not two weeks ago."

"Took off?" Mary stared blankly at Luke.

"They gave up. Took off. Went home to where they come from. After—"

"Went home?" echoed Mary.

"It was after—" Luke began again.

Mary put out her hand as if to stop the words she knew were coming next, words she had known she would have to hear from the day Kirsty Mackay had died, the day her headache had stopped. Then, because she could not bear to hear this stranger speak them, she said them herself.

"It was after Duncan died," she said.

CHAPTER V
I Am Alone Here

Luke Anderson took Mary to the house next to the mill. "Julia Colliver will take care of you," he assured her. Mary sat unmoving in the cart, not feeling the heat, the sweat pouring down her face, the gnats swarming around her, the flies and mosquitoes settling on her. When a large, middle-aged woman came out of the house and put out her hand for her, Mary obediently stepped down.

"Come along, child, we'll have a nice cup of the tea Luke's brought us off the boat at Soames."

Mary sat by the table in the kitchen of the Collivers' house with the cup and saucer in front of her.

"They never give a thought to leaving their place, neither Davie nor Jean, when the baby—little Iain—took sick of the dysentery. But after Duncan...." Mrs. Colliver sighed and shook her

head. "Well, the heart just sort of went out of them.
There wasn't nothing anybody could say would
make them change their minds. They left without a
stick of furniture, only her spinning wheel. The
four of 'em looked so beat down when they took off
from here it was enough to make your own heart
bleed. They was good folks, though they wasn't just
the same as us, and we'll miss them sorely." Mrs.
Colliver talked on and on but Mary didn't hear any
more. Nor did she notice when the cup of cold tea
was taken away.

Luke Anderson left. Sam Colliver came in from
the mill. The children came and whispered around
her. She did not hear them. Mrs. Colliver led her to
a bed. She went without protest.

She lay there for three days and nights. In the
middle of the fourth night she started, terrified,
from a dream in which Duncan was calling. She did
not know where she was or how she had got there.

She could see that she was in a bed and that there
was a window opposite. She got up, tripped over
the voluminous night-gown she was wearing, and
tiptoed to the window. The moon was nearly full
and after a moment or two she could make out a
clearing, an outbuilding of some sort, a road, and
beyond it the huge oaks, maples, elms, and evergreens of the forest. The familiar hollow sound of
an owl's hoot and the fragrance of mint and roses
comforted her.

She shifted her gaze back to the room. It was
small with a floor of wide boards scrubbed white,
plastered walls, and a low, beamed ceiling. A door
in the wall adjacent to the window led into the next

room. She pulled the night-dress to her knees and went through the door.

She was in the kitchen. There was a fireplace and a bake oven along one wall, windows opposite, and at the back another window and two doors. There was a large dresser full of plates beside the window, and in the middle of the room was a long table with benches along either side, and a chair at either end. Behind the kitchen was a scullery. Beyond the kitchen at the front of the house was another room; beside that, the front door and a hall and the stairs to a second storey. Across the hall was another room.

Mary crept around the front room and back into the kitchen as carefully as a cat. She peered through the back window, then the side window. From there she could see the road that went past the front of the house. At once she remembered Luke Anderson. She remembered the village. She remembered all that Julia Colliver had told her. A wave of dizziness swept over her, and she clutched the low window-sill to steady herself. She slumped to the floor and put her head on the sill.

"I came here as fast as I could, *mo gràdach*. On wings I would have flown but I had none. Och, Duncan, however will I live my whole lifetime without you?"

The dizziness passed leaving such anguish that Mary could not move or think or even weep. Slowly the Gaelic mourning words began inside her, "*och-on, och-on,*" chanting themselves over and over until she grew calm.

Outside a rooster began to crow. Not long afterwards daylight came and she heard the Colliver family beginning to get up. Stiffly she stood as one by one they came into the kitchen. She answered politely that she was feeling better and took her turn in the outside privy and at the well in the back yard with the seven children. Ignoring their stares and whispers, she went back to the room where she had slept. Both her shawls had been hung up on pegs by the door. Everything else had been laundered, smoothed with a smoothing iron, folded, and placed neatly on the small ladder-backed chair that stood just inside the door—not only the clothes Mrs. Babbington had given her but her old threadbare ones. The spindle whorl and Mrs. Grant's letter had been laid on top of the pile. Without hesitating she put on her old shift and skirt. Then she combed her hair, pulled the bright coverlet over the bedclothes, and sat down on top, unsure what she should do next.

Through the open door she could see Julia Colliver bustling about, hear her giving orders to the children. Julia Colliver was definitely a large woman. She was large-bodied with large hands and feet and a large head distinguished by a mass of grey-brown hair wound into a neat knot at her neck. Her brown eyes were large too, and round, and so was her face. Her nose was broad and her mouth was full. Not only her proportions but her way of moving in sure, wide movements bespoke an authoritative but generous nature. If the house had been a simple cottage or Julia a trifle less imposing Mary would have gone to offer help, but the only other house she had been in with more than one room in it had been Tigh na shuidh, where she had been a kitchen maid so briefly.

"This is not so grand as that," she decided, "but it is grand indeed, and so clean!" She slid her bare foot back and forth along the smooth boards and wondered if Aunt Jean and Uncle Davie had had such a fine house.

One of the small girls called shyly through the door, "Ma says it's breakfast time."

Breakfast was an orderly affair in the Colliver household. Before the children sat down in two rows at the table, their hands, faces, and ears had to pass their mother's inspection. Their crockery bowls and plates were placed before them, their father, a small, neat man, said grace, and only then were they permitted to dip their spoons into their porridge and maple sugar.

Mary, seated beside the biggest girl, watched carefully to see how she managed and was relieved to discover that eating was the same in Upper Canada as it was in the north of Scotland, even though the porridge was made of ground Indian corn. During a lull in the noisy talk, she said, "Mr. and Mrs. Colliver, it is very good to me you have been and I thank you for it. I will not ever forget."

"Oh, dearie, don't you think on it any more." Mrs. Colliver's large, round face radiated kindness. "We was awful worried these last few days. You was lying there all pale and you so little and skinny. Why, the whole neighbourhood's been in to see how you was doing. Luke Anderson's been around every day. We could all see it was a terrible shock learning the bad news, and then to find out the others had up and left.... Why, I just can't fancy Jean and Davie Cameron going off like that when you was coming to stay."

"They did not know."

"Oh, then you just come from somewhere in the province? You ain't come all the way from Scotland."

"I have."

"All that way? Without them knowing you was coming?"

"I have." Mary replied stiffly. She was somewhat taken aback by the questioning.

"All that way! Have you...are you...are your folks all right?"

"They are well. I came because—because I heard Duncan call. I had to come."

"You heard him call? But you was in Scotland." Mrs. Colliver stared uncomprehendingly at Mary.

Reluctantly, Mary admitted, "I heard because I have the two sights."

Still Mrs. Colliver looked blank.

Mary was puzzled. "It was because I have the two sights. Do you have a different word for that? Sometimes I see the past, sometimes the future. Sometimes I see the distance—it is the unseen world. We say it is the two sights."

"Can you see ghosts?" Seven-year-old Nancy, shyness overcome, tugged excitedly at Mary's sleeve. The other children stopped eating and turned to her in awe.

"Is that what you mean? Ghosts?" Mrs. Colliver was incredulous.

"I do not—och, those too." Mary began to twist a strand of her hair nervously around her finger, something she had not done for years.

"We don't hold with ghosts or any of that nonsense," Mrs. Colliver said firmly. "Seems to me

God's got plenty on his hands taking care of us living, without sending us the dead to deal with. And you might be better off, young woman, seeing how strange you was took, if you didn't think like that neither."

It was Mary's turn to stare. What could Mrs. Colliver mean? "Don't hold with ghosts"? Ghosts were ghosts as the living were the living. It hadn't anything to do with how you felt about them or how you thought God felt about them. Was Mrs. Colliver playing a joke? No, Mrs. Colliver was clearly not that kind of a woman. Why would she say such things then?

"There now, don't you fret, my girl, you'll be all right." Mrs. Colliver reached over and patted Mary's arm.

Sam got up from the table. "Listen to Julia." He smiled broadly at Mary. "You'll be all right with us. Don't you fret," and he was off out the door. Later Mary realized that those were the only words, other than the saying of the grace, she had heard Sam Colliver utter. She wondered, fleetingly, if Sam ever got much chance to talk.

The children began to gabble noisily. Now and then Nancy or Matthew or Robert, the smaller ones, looked sideways at Mary but none of them approached her. Their mother and one of the older girls got up to clear the table and the young ones went outside. Mary followed them.

Although it was only seven in the morning the day was already hot and muggy, the air thick with insects. Otherwise the village seemed a cheerful place. The Collivers' house was as pleasant outside as in. It was made of boards stained a rich, soft, red and seemed to Mary quite elegant. There were one or two other houses made of frame and one of stone. The rest were the log cabins she had become used to seeing.

Behind the Collivers' house was a yard, mostly cleared of stumps and planted with some kind of enormous-leafed vines.

"Them's squashes and pumpkins," Nancy, the smallest, told her. "We eats the miserable things all winter."

Beyond the yard and to the east was a log out-building. The byre, Mary figured. The children called it the barn. There was a path from the house to the barn and from there to the road. Around it, on all sides, were small fields still full of stumps. Not more than a hundred yards behind them the woods began. About as far to the east were another log barn and a house. "Miz Hazen's store," Matthew told her. Immediately to the west were the stream and the mill.

In front of the house was a small patch of garden. Mary recognized turnips, beans, potatoes, and onions. There were also a few flowers, herbs, and more vegetables she did not know all growing in neat, well-cultivated rows. Along one edge of the garden, uprooted stumps made a strange-looking fence. The other three sides were surrounded by dark red, crudely woven withies.

"Ma says they make dandy fences, them dog-woods. Cows can't get over and pigs can't get through, but they ain't as lasty as the stumps," Matthew told her importantly.

Chickens and ducks and geese had no trouble making their way into the garden. They were clucking and quacking and scrabbling busily among the plants. Perched on the ridge-pole of the barn, the rooster proclaimed his unceasing cru-curu-curu to the world, the sharp sound of it echoed by other roosters on other ridge-poles up and down the road.

Across the way, in the woods, a few unfamiliar songbirds chirped listlessly in the heat. The big passenger pigeons purretted from low branches and now and again a crow caw-cawed.

Above it all Mary could feel, almost more than she heard, the steady soughing of the wind through the high branches of the great trees. For a long time she stood by the dogwood fence looking across at the forest. Finally she whispered a word of prayer, encircled the spindle whorl in her pocket with her hand, crossed the road, and stepped purposefully into the woods. A series of deep, uncontrollable shudders pulsed through her. She fell back as though she had been struck and fled towards the house.

Mrs. Colliver was coming from the back yard. "Whoa! You're safe now, girl. There, there." She put her arms around Mary's trembling body. "It ain't too smart to just charge into the woods alone without knowing where you're going. Was it a bear?"

Mary's eyes were wide with fright and her breath still came in ragged gasps. She pulled away from Mrs. Colliver and sat down on the front step of the house. "I cannot stay here! I cannot!" The words burst from her. "I must go home. I will go now, this very day."

"Steady, girl. You can't just up and go home without money to get you there. You stay here with us a while. You can help with the chores for your room and board and, if you want, you can weave and spin along with me to earn the money to get you home. Now, I earned us a whole parcel of land by my weaving and—"

"I will go as I came, trusting in God to find the means."

"Oh!" Mrs. Colliver's eyebrows shot towards her hairline. She put her hands on her hips. "Well, mebbe God will give you a hand, my girl, but it's a sight more likely you'll run afoul of the Devil."

Matthew sniggered.

"That'll do, Matthew. Now, no matter how hot it is we got to get the hoeing done and you might as well give a hand, Mary. Here, I brung you out a sunbonnet—now don't argue with me. I remember Jean Cameron when she first come here with her neat little white bonnet. She wasn't going to wear nothing like this but it wasn't long before she had one on her head same as the rest of us. I reckon you don't get a particular amount of sun back where you come from. Here now, children, come along—Matthew, Solomon, Deborah, Nancy, Susan!"

Reduced to silence—and obedience—by the deluge of words and the force of Julia Colliver's personality, Mary took the sunbonnet and meekly followed the parade to the barn for hoes. As she worked the rows with the strange, straight-handled hoe, she brooded over what Julia had said. She felt rebuked by the words "work for your room and board". The Colliver family had been so good to her. They had taken her in without a word and treated her so kindly that she felt a great obligation to repay them. But when she thought of staying in this dark, flat land, this place that held only grief for her, she felt cold and scared. When she thought of the long, dangerous trip home, she felt almost worse.

"Mother! Mrs. Grant! What shall I do?" her heart cried out as she worked, and more than one potato and turnip plant were slashed by the heavy blows of her hoe.

The gardening hadn't more than begun when a big, fair-haired girl came bounding up the road, braids bouncing, arms waving wildly. Her sunbonnet swung precariously from one hand, in the other a half-grown chicken huddled against the reckless motion.

"I brung you the pullet Ma promised on account of Mose stepping on yours," she shouted as she pushed through the gate. "I—oh, I thought you was Sally. Oh, I guess you're Mary who Luke brought from Scotland—I don't mean he brought you all the way from there, I mean—oh, well, I'm Patty Openshaw from over by Hawthorn Bay and I'm right sorry how things landed out for you."

Patty had a pretty pink face and bright blue eyes but what was most instantly noticeable about her was that she was dressed in bright blue from her bonnet to her boots and that she seemed to be always in motion, bouncing, bounding, and jumping around as she talked. As well she seemed bold to Mary—bold in what she said, bold in what she asked. But then, the Canadians all seemed bold to Mary in the direct way they spoke and quizzed each other.

"You come all this way to see your folks and Duncan's dead and the others are gone off home. Ain't that sad? Oh, here, Debbie, Matt, what's your ma doing? Someone take this darn-blasted chicken before she scratches the skin right off my hand."

The chicken was squawking and flapping and doing its best to escape. Grinning delightedly, Matthew took it by its legs and ran into the house to show his mother. Seconds later he was scooted through the door by Mrs. Colliver.

"Get that dirty thing outta my house," she stormed. "Oh hello, Patty. I was meaning to send down to ask if you could give us a hand pretty soon."

"I'll come days Ma don't need me but you know how Ma is sure to see disaster around the corner waiting if any of us is two steps from the house. What she's gonna do when we all leave home, I don't know."

"Well, you ask her right sweetly for me."

"I will and maybe," she swung around to face Mary, "if you've a mind, you could come on down and visit a spell with me." She smiled broadly and was off in a swirl of blue strings flying from the bonnet now loosely tied under her chin.

While they washed onions in the scullery for dinner Mrs. Colliver continued her morning's monologue. "I'd like fine for you to stop here with us a spell, Mary. Gran died last year and our Sal's just gotten married and what with preserving season coming on soon I could use another pair of hands. The boys ain't much help with that kind of work and, besides, their pa needs the big ones over to the mill. The little girls is too little. Hired girl got married too." There was a note in Mrs. Colliver's voice that suggested hired girls had no business getting married.

"Patty Openshaw's a good worker but she does flap some and she's a mite easygoing. You seems a good, strong girl." Mrs. Colliver gave the young green onions a vigorous shake and put them on the platter with a pile of boiled potatoes and slices of cold pork.

Mary could see that Mrs. Colliver did need someone to help. But Mrs. Colliver was telling her straight out what she should do and she didn't like it. Nevertheless the sense of obligation hung over her. She wiped her wet hands on her borrowed apron and picked up the platter. "I will help you," she said. She carried the platter to the table, marvelling at the quantity of meat.

That night she dreamed again that Duncan was calling her. In the dream she could see him so clearly, black hair hanging over a dark face contorted with pain, and hear his voice growing louder and louder, "Mairi! Mairi! Mairi!"

"Wait for me, Duncan!" she cried and began to run fast, faster, without getting anywhere. As she moved forward at last, she was overcome by such dread that she woke up, strangling a scream in her throat. She was halfway out of bed.

Her heart pounding, she sat on the edge of the bed. "Duncan, you have gone where I cannot go."

She pushed her heavy, hot hair from her face and rubbed her eyes. She felt so far from home, so far from her own people, so far from her own heather-covered hills.

The next few days Mary hoed and weeded and helped with meals, too stunned, too unhappy, to think about what she was going to do.

"My land, you don't seem very handy in a kitchen for such a big girl. You'll want a heap of learning before you'll make any man much of a wife," Mrs. Colliver grumbled at her.

After a few days Mary took on the care of the farm animals. For that work Mrs. Colliver had only praise. In fact she bragged to all her neighbours that there was "twice the number of eggs and twice the yield of milk since Mary Urkit come." In the evenings the small children came to Mary to be told stories, to listen to her "queer talk", and to bring her their chronicles of the day's events.

But the nights were a torment. She dreamed the same dream of Duncan over and over again, always waking in fright. One night she woke stumbling along the road in the dark, far from the house, calling out, "Wait for me!"

Still shaking from the nightmare, she thought at first that she was still asleep. Then she realized that she was wearing Julia Colliver's oversized nightdress. It was several minutes before she figured out where she was.

She sat down on a boulder beside the road to calm herself. The air was hot and heavy and so still there was no sound from the treetops. The sudden bark of a fox, the hoot of an owl deep in the woods seemed as close as the gurrup of the frogs and the rusty crik-crik of the crickets on the roadside. Mary shivered.

"The woods are worse than the nightmare," she said aloud.

"Is it someone?" a voice quavered from behind her. Mary leapt to her feet. She stood in the middle of the road, her hands at her throat.

"Is someone there?" the voice pleaded. It wasn't much more than a whisper.

"It is Mairi Urquhart. Who is there?"

"Henry."

"Come out then, Henry."

Within seconds a small, spindly boy appeared from the woods. His eyes were large and scared. His thin face was black with tears and dirt. His hair hung limp. His clothes, what Mary could see of them, looked filthy and ragged. He was the most woebegone creature she had ever seen.

"Henry," she demanded, "where did you come from?"

"In there."

"Do you live there?"

"No, miss."

"What were you doing in there?"

He burst into tears. "Sim said he was gonna skin me for taking his hat and I run off and then I got lost."

By now Mary's own fears had quietened. "Why did you take Sim's hat?" she asked softly.

"I needed it for the bird."

"Ah."

"It was sick."

"Did it get better?"

"It died."

"In Sim's hat?"

"Yes. It was my friend." Henry began to cry again. Through his sobs he managed to tell Mary that the bird was a crow he had rescued from an owl earlier in the summer. As a result of the owl's attack, it had never been able to fly. "And," Henry finished, "it got et by a fox. I seen its miserable red tail."

"So you buried what there was left in the hat?"

He nodded, unable to stifle the sobs.

Mary sat Henry beside her on the big rock where she had perched herself earlier and told him of the time she and Duncan had found a bird. "An owl, I fear, Henry." She looked at him. "It was a wee, downy, white thing and, Henry, a wee thing is a wee thing and you must love it. We did not take it home for we knew where its mother had the nest—in a hollow in a bit of old heather not far from where we was—so we left it and said the words over it that the mother would not fear our scent. We went back the next day and it was not there nor any sign of feathers to say some beast had caught it. We was glad."

"Yes." Henry's tears had dried, his sobs had stopped. The sky was lightening over the treetops. "I can see where we are," he cried joyfully. "We're just up the road from the mill, up by the Corners." Without another word, he sprang to his feet and ran back into the woods.

Much relieved herself, Mary saw the tall outlines of the Collivers' mill not three hundred yards down the road. "I hope Sim does not beat Henry," she thought as she made her way up the road.

Outside the house she stopped to look again at the forest across the road. "I fear this place. I fear its evil spirits. May the old ones who dwell in this country be friendly to me and help me to get home."

Not half an hour later a small boy pounded on the kitchen door.

"Ma's took bad. Pa says will the missus please come."

Mrs. Colliver began at once to give orders to Mary, to the children, to her husband, as she got ready to leave. A second knock came. It was Luke Anderson.

"It's baby," he told them. "It's awful sick. Ma'd take it kindly if Miz Colliver could lend a hand."

"I can't, Luke. I'm just readying myself up to go off to Jenny Heaton." Mrs. Colliver paused, looked doubtfully at Mary. She sighed. "Mary, you'll have to go. Sam and the young ones can look after themselves. My land, what kind of a bad-luck day is this?"

Mary did not move from where she stood by the fireplace. Everyone was looking at her. Another moment passed.

"You'll just have to go, Mary," Mrs. Colliver repeated. "Pack up your clothes. You may be a day or two."

"I will go." Mary tied her spare clothes in a bundle and followed Luke out the door.

CHAPTER VI
Baby

The finches and waxwings were chirping and calling fitfully through the trees as Mary and Luke set off. The patch of sky visible above the road was grey and hazy.

"I guess you're feeling a mite better now you been here a while." Luke's voice was friendly. Mary nodded.

"Julia Colliver's a good woman," he said.

Again Mary nodded.

"You're all right there?"

"I am."

Luke gave up his attempt at conversation and they tramped along silently until he headed into the woods. "Short cut," he explained.

"I will not go there," Mary declared flatly.

"We'll be all right. It's broad daylight. The bears

won't bother you none unless you go after their cubs and the other fellers—the foxes and lynxes and wolves—will run at the sound of you. We always cut through here. The Indians blazed the trail for us—a while back, I guess.''

Mary did not budge.

"Come on." Luke spoke firmly but gently, as though coaxing a small child or a frightened calf. Still Mary did not move.

Luke frowned. "I'm gonna head through the woods. You can walk around if you've a mind to.'' He started off again. Mary marched briskly up the road ten paces, eleven paces. The crackling of dry leaves and twigs under Luke's feet ceased.

"You ain't coming," he called, astonished.

"I am not." Mary marched on. In a moment Luke had caught up with her and they continued without speaking. Although she was strong and well accustomed to walking, Mary had to work to keep up to Luke's long-legged, purposeful gait. Now and then she felt him look at her and she wished he wouldn't. She had a feeling he was laughing at her.

"Like a great urisk, he is," she thought crossly. It was believed in the Highlands that the big, awkward, shy goat-man lurked behind the high rocks to play jokes on people. Mary was sure she had seen its shadow at least once. Searching for a lost lamb on a summer's night near the shieling, scrambling high up into the crevices of the highest rocks where lambs so love to climb, she had seen a huge black shadow. For an instant the hair on her neck and down her back had prickled in fear before she realized it must be the urisk, although as she said later she had seen "not an ear of him''.

"Urisk," she had called softly, so as not to alarm or offend him, "Urisk, it is the wee *uan* that has got himself lost. I would sing a song of gladness for that wee *uan*." There had been no response, but not three minutes later the lamb had appeared from behind the rocks. Mary had sung her song and, ever after, had stopped by that outcropping to hum or sing to the urisk.

Luke was not awkward and Mary had no reason to believe he was stupid. He was big, however, just under six feet tall. He had a round face, bright brown eyes, a snub nose, and a wide mouth. His thick chestnut-coloured hair looked as though it had been cut with a knife. Not handsome, he had a warmth and kindliness to him that made him pleasing to look at. As well, he had an air of determination—or stubbornness—that spoke of capability. And in spite of the fact that his pants were none too clean and hung from a single suspender, and his shirt badly needed mending, he had a neat look. He certainly did not look like a goat-man.

A picture came to her of Luke carrying a small boy. She could not see the child, as his back was to her, but the expression on Luke's face was so distraught that instinctively Mary turned and put her hand on his arm. The picture disappeared. She shook herself.

"The skitters and midges are fierce." Luke smiled sympathetically. When he smiled it was with his whole body—from his warm brown eyes to his big, broad feet. Hastily Mary withdrew her hand.

They had walked three miles when Luke turned off the government road onto a narrower one, not much more than a path through the woods. Mary thought of her horrible flight along such a path the night she had walked from Cornwall. She shivered and halted.

"It's the only way to get there." Luke looked down at her. He grinned. "You want I should carry you the rest of the way?"

Mary blushed. "I do not mind the road." She stalked ahead. Luke stuffed his hands into the pockets of his pants and began to whistle.

In single file, preceded by the nervous scolding of the finches and bobolinks and small animals, the two made their way over a log bridge, up a rise, and along the path for five more miles to the Anderson homestead.

"Here it is." Luke pushed open the door and led the way into the house. From somewhere in the smoky room there was a loud laugh. "Ain't much good bringing us a itty-bitty little stick like that, Luke."

No one else said anything. A cat mewed.

All Mary could think of was the seven weeks she had spent on the *Andrew MacBride*. It was the stench and the small dark space. As her eyes adjusted to the dim light, she saw two boys sitting at the table in the centre of the room. One was a large, red-haired, red-faced boy, more or less her own age. The other was Henry. A woman sat by the smouldering fire in a rocking-chair. In spite of the suffocating heat she was huddled under a large shawl.

"This here's Mary." Luke took Mary's arm and drew her into the room. "Miz Colliver's off nursing Miz Heaton."

"Can't be helped, I expect." The woman sighed plaintively. "Git the jug for the girl, Sim."

"Good morning to you, Henry," said Mary.

Henry dipped his head shyly but made no sound. His brother poured from a large jug into a battered pewter cup. He lumbered across the room.

"Here y'are, have a good swig. Helps the bugs." He laughed.

It was whisky. Mary had only ever had whisky in small measures. Her mother and father had brought it out at the feast of Beltane, at New Year, at births, funerals, or for chills. She was tempted, all the same, to gulp down the entire contents of the cup.

"Sim, Mary don't want no—" Luke began.

"You shut your mouth!" Sim glared.

Just then a big, red-haired man burst through the door. "Which one a you young apes left the white-faced cow on the other side of the road untethered?" he bellowed. "She's calved in the swamp and I can't find the goddamn calf nowheres."

"Please, John, don't swear," Mrs. Anderson whimpered.

John Anderson let loose a stream of words only a few of which Mary had ever heard before, and those only by chance. Mrs. Anderson sniffed. Sim roared with laughter. "I don't need no lip outta you, Simeon Anderson. Git yourself—and you others too—out there and find that calf." His father reached across the table, lifted the whisky jug to his mouth, gulped from it as though it held spring water, turned on his heel, and left the house. Simeon, Luke, and Henry followed.

Still holding the whisky Sim had given her, Mary stared, mesmerized, at Mrs. Anderson drooping in her chair. From the corner the cat mewed again.

"Would you mind fetching me a drop from the jug, honey? I been feeling poorly since the baby come."

Mary took the woman the pewter cup. The mewing in the corner grew louder.

"Oh, do see to baby." Mrs. Anderson lifted her hand to push back the lank, fair hair from her face, then sank back into her chair. Mary realized, with shock, that what she had thought was a cat was the baby.

He was in a box in the corner behind Mrs. Anderson's chair. As she looked at him Mary saw the grey mist of death around him. She sighed. He was thin and as blue-white as skimmed milk. He was wet and dirty and wrapped only in an old matted shawl. Flies clustered around his face.

"Och, the poor wee *uan*," murmured Mary as she lifted the baby from the box. "Come, come," she crooned. She rocked him until he had stopped his wailing, too weak, too ill to go on—too weak, too ill to raise his fist more than halfway to his mouth.

"He must be hungry," she told Mrs. Anderson indignantly, "and he needs a clean cloth. Because he is dying is no reason to leave him like this."

"Don't talk like that, honey. I don't know what's to be done. We allus gets Miz Whitcomb to come. She knows. She knows what…." Mrs. Anderson closed her eyes, her voice trailed off into a thin snore, and her head fell back against the chair.

Rocking the baby on her arm, Mary searched the cabin in vain for a clean cloth. "Nor is she likely to have a drop of milk in her to give the poor wee

76

mite," she muttered angrily, "and had she one it would surely be all whisky." She opened all the crocks and jugs in the cupboard, hoping to find milk. "For," she reasoned, "they have a cow."

"Please, miss."

Mary jumped, whirled around, and all but dropped the baby. It was Henry. He looked scared but he stood his ground.

"Would you send us all into the arms of Auld Clutie before he has made ready for us in hell?" she cried.

"Please, miss," he repeated, "Emily's freshened if you wants milk fer baby."

"I do." Mary nodded and Henry ran off. He was back in a few minutes with a small crockery bowl full of warm milk. Mary dipped her finger into it then put the finger in the baby's mouth. He sucked it feebly. She did it two or three times more, then he turned his face, too tired to suck.

"Henry, the bairnie is needing water and a nappie. Is there a scrap of cloth we might get?"

Without a word Henry went to a box under a bed in a corner of the room and brought out a rag. He ran outside and came back with it dripping wet.

"Is there not a wee dishie?"

He looked puzzled.

"A dishie like this with the milk in it."

He went to the cupboard, brought out a wooden trencher, was off again, and brought it back full of water. Mary took the baby closer to the fire where there were fewer bugs. She took off his dirty rags and sponged him off as best she could. He scarcely made a sound.

Henry brought another rag which Mary wrapped around the baby for a diaper. She did not want to put him back into the same dirty shawl in which she had found him but she could find no other clean cloth in the entire cabin. Tight-jawed, she crossed the room, grabbed her bundle from beside the door, hauled out her clean shift, and tore it in half. Back she went and folded it tenderly around the baby.

"What name has he?" she asked Henry.

"He don't got a name."

"No name?"

"Nobody got to it yet, I guess."

"Well, the poor, wee thing, to have no name at all."

"Will he die?"

"He will."

Henry said no more. Under Mary's instructions he put the box by the fire and while she cradled the baby in her arms, walking slowly around and around as she had walked with so many sick lambs, she sang him a lullaby in her own language.

After a time John Anderson came in with the older boys close behind him. "You young scoundrel!" He cuffed Henry sharply on the back of his head. "You—" He noticed Mary. "Who the hell are you?" he growled.

The baby let out a shrill cry. Mrs. Anderson started up in her chair.

"I am Mairi Urquhart, come from Collivers' Corner to—"

"Speak up, gal, speak up. I guess you come to help. Ain't much to be done for the kid. Ain't much to be done about anything." He went to the cupboard, brushed the flies from a chunk of cold cooked pork, cut himself a thick slice, picked up a boiled potato, and went back outside.

"Crazy old man," muttered Sim.

"Did you find it, Lukey?" whispered Henry.

"Yeah, we found it," Luke answered tiredly.

"Is it dead?"

"Naw," Luke grinned, "nice little white heifer. It's outside by its ma."

Henry went outside. Luke looked at the baby asleep in Mary's arms. "Ain't you good!" he said. "Have you et?"

Involuntarily Mary's eyes darted towards the fly-covered meat on the cupboard. "I am not hungry," she replied quickly. Luke flushed and went back outside. Simeon grabbed some meat and followed.

Wishing she hadn't hurt Luke's feelings, Mary resumed her rocking and walking. The baby whimpered and she began to hum, thinking again, as she had done when nursing Kirsty Mackay's baby on board ship, that babies were not so different from lambs. "I will call you Uan Beg, which means, in your language, tiny lamb."

The baby clung to life all through the day. But that night he died.

CHAPTER VII
Fire

Mary stayed at the Andersons' for the burying. It was not the custom in the Highlands for women to attend burials but this was in a little square of ground at the edge of the clearing just behind the house. John Anderson did not bring the neighbours in to help or to mourn. He put together a tiny cedar box. Mary washed the baby, chanted a song for the dead over him, wrapped him in the two pieces of her linen shift, and put him in the box.

Mrs. Anderson kept back by the house. Mary stood by the grave with Henry's hand held tightly in hers. There was no preacher to come as there was none in the district. John Anderson, such a different man than he had seemed the night before, read the Twenty-third Psalm from the family Bible in a deep, quiet voice and they all recited the Lord's

Prayer. Carefully Luke and Simeon put the box in the hole they had dug, covered it with earth, and left the baby beside the five other Anderson infants who had not survived their first year.

Mr. Anderson had just closed the Bible when a small, grey-haired woman came tramping briskly up the road with a basket on her arm. She took in the scene with one sweeping glance, crossed the yard, and stood for a moment beside the new grave with her head bowed. She took Mr. Anderson's hand. "It's hard losing a baby," she said quietly, "as we all know well, but you and Lydia have lost too many." She clasped the boys' hands one by one, nodded towards Mary, and went at once to where Mrs. Anderson leaned against the back of the house.

"Come, Lydia," she said gently. "We'll find some coffee and fix things up a mite for you." Like a lost child, Mrs. Anderson gave the woman her hand and went with her into the house.

"Miz Whitcomb will likely get you something to eat, boys," Mr. Anderson said wearily and he went across the road, picked up his axe, and began to swing it fiercely at the base of the nearest tree.

Mary sat down on a big stump near the door of the cabin. Suddenly she began to weep.

"What are you bawling about? Miz Whitcomb'll put out a good feed. Come on." Sim had already recovered from the awe and sadness of the burial.

His words made her tears come faster. She could not stop them. She wept noisily, in great sobs.

Luke knelt beside her. He put his hand awkwardly on her shoulder. "The little mite hadn't no more than just opened his eyes."

"I know. And I did know he would die." Mary could not tell him that it was not only the baby, it was also Kirsty Mackay and it was Duncan.

Luke got up and went into the house. He was back promptly with a mug in one hand and a slice of bread and some cheese in the other.

"Here's coffee. Dandelion root. Miz Whitcomb brung it. And I got some grub, too. Eat it, you'll feel better. You ain't et a thing since you come here yesterday."

Sniffing and gulping back her sobs, Mary drank some of the coffee. It was bitter but it was hot and comforting. She took a bite of the bread and cheese, realizing with surprise that she was very hungry. She did not look up until she had finished. "Is there more?" she asked.

Henry, who had been watching her every bite, ran to get it. Luke grinned, obviously relieved. Mary saw that he had been afraid she would retreat into herself as she had done when he had told her Duncan was dead. She smiled weakly. Henry returned with another slice of bread and cheese for her while Luke went to get his own breakfast. Henry sat down on the ground near Mary.

"Will you stay here with us?"

"Och! I cannot do that, but I will not go while you eat your meal."

Watching her from the corner of his eye, Henry went into the house. She was not there when he came back out. It wasn't more than two minutes after he had gone that Mary had a clear premonition of a barn on fire. With it came a compulsion to warn someone, a compulsion that always accompanied such visions. She didn't know whose barn it was, but she knew that if she started out, her feet would take her there.

She forced herself, against the pull of every nerve in her body, to sit still. "It is not my country. I will not go. These people do not know I have the two sights. I do not need to let them know." But the compulsion to run and warn set her on her feet even as she pronounced the words. She looked around, frantic for some means of keeping herself from racing off. Her eyes fell on the privy off behind the cabin.

"Nobody will quiz me about that!" She ran towards it as though all the devils in hell were after her, slammed the door shut, and shoved the wooden bolt across it.

"What a dreadful place." She shuddered. The privy stank, the flies were buzzing noisily, a large grass snake wriggled off between the floorboards. The only fresh air came from a slot above the door. Her feet not quite touching the floor, Mary sat on the edge of the seat, clinging to it with both hands, willing herself not to touch the bolt. From a distance she heard Henry call. She heard Luke and Simeon come out of the house, heard Simeon say, "Shut up, Henry. The gal's run off. Didn't like our company, I guess." And Luke: "I expect she had enough sadness. Come on, Henry, she ain't left the face of the earth, she's only took off for the Collivers'. We'll go see her after supper if you want."

Henry made no reply. Before long the ringing sound of John's axe against the tree was joined by the chorus of Luke's and Simeon's axes. Closer by, there was the scritch, scritch of a hoe. Mary was sure it was Henry working among the pumpkins and squash.

After five more minutes the stink, combined with the stuffy heat in the privy and her overpowering urge to warn of the fire, were too much. Mary slid back the bolt and pushed against the door. It did not open. She pushed again. Still it did not open. She leaned against it with all her strength. It did not budge. She climbed on the seat, stood on tiptoe, and put her hand through the opening over the door in order to reach down to whatever was holding the door shut. She could not get her arm down far enough.

She shouted for help but the sound of the axes was too loud. Finally she gave up and slumped down on the seat. "I need not worry about the fire, then," she thought, and after a time, exhausted from her efforts and the wakeful night, she fell asleep.

Hours later, when the sun no longer streamed through the slot above the privy door, she woke. Outside there wasn't a sound. She climbed up on the seat and peered out. The axes stood against a fresh stump. A tiny, sleek, squirrel-like animal with stripes along its back was sitting on the stump, washing itself. There wasn't a person in sight. She began to shout. No one answered.

"It is nothing but a wooden door, surely I can get out through it," she thought crossly. She put her hand through the slot and reached down until her arm was on the outside up to her shoulder with the rest of her on tiptoe inside.

Janet Lunn

From somewhere near there was a cry. Mary
pulled her arm in and began to shout loudly for
help. At first there was no response. Then she heard
Simeon: "Don't be a simpleton, Henry. There's no
one in there. No one but Ma uses it in summer."

"You gotta come and look, Sim. I seen an arm
sticking out of it. Honest."

"Henry, you're a—" The door was flung open.
"Well, I'll be dang-blasted!"

"Thank you," said Mary. She hopped down from
the seat and shoved past him into the bright afternoon sun.

"I told you I was not going away while you ate
your meal, Henry," she snapped.

"I'm sorry," whispered Henry. He shot off across
the front yard before Mary could say another word.

By this time Simeon had recovered from his surprise and was hooting with laughter. "In the honey
box," he shouted, pointing his finger at Mary. "In
the honey box. All afternoon. You'd a been there all
night, too, if I hadn't got you out. What am I gonna
get for my pains, Miss Uppity? Come on, let's have
a kiss." He leaned over her. She drew back.

"May you grow garlic in your chin whiskers,
Simeon Anderson, and an onion on your ugly red
nose!"

Simeon's hand flew to his nose. "Ha!" He
laughed, embarrassed by his action. "What did you
say that for? What a queer skinny little gal you are.
You talk funny, you act funny, but I want my kiss
anyways."

Mary thrust his arm from her and started off
across the yard. At that moment, Luke rounded the
corner of the house with Henry in his arms.

"It was Henry. Dear Lord, it was Henry," Mary cried. "I saw! It was when we were walking through the woods. I saw you but I did not see it was Henry. I did not realize...."

"He's fell out of a tree." Luke's usually cheerful face was grim.

Henry was unconscious. Luke and Simeon laid him on his bed. Mary took charge. While they looked on she felt all his bones carefully. He had broken a bone in one leg, and probably sprained one wrist. He had also had a severe knock on his head. But everything else seemed all right.

Simeon left. Mrs. Anderson had gone to bed. Mrs. Whitcomb had gone home. Frantically Mary searched her memory for what to do. How she wished now that she had been willing to learn all Mrs. Grant had wanted to teach her about healing. There were a few things she could bring to mind and, with Luke to fetch what she needed, she made a poultice of egg whites and cornmeal for Henry's head, muttering all the while that it should have been barley. For a splint for the break Luke found two straight sticks and wound lengths torn from Henry's own shirt around them.

"Are there eels to be had in this country?" Mary remembered Mrs. Grant wrapping eel skins around her own ankle when she had sprained it falling down a badger hole.

"Eels?"

"Fishes—long, thin, snaky fishes."

"I know what eels are."

"Then will you please catch me two as fast as you can."

"It's gonna take a bit of time. I gotta get to the lake and. . . ."

"Luke, two eels, I must have two eels."

"All right." Still eyeing her uneasily, Luke went off to do her bidding.

Mary straightened up at last, noticing for the first time that Mrs. Whitcomb had washed all the dishes, swept the dirt floor, laundered the clothes, and put some kind of order into the house. The table was set with plates, mugs, and inviting-looking humps hidden under cloths to keep the flies off. Under the cloths were a bowl of cold potatoes, a platter of freshly boiled sliced pork, a loaf of bread, and a bowl of butter.

"So much meat in this country," breathed Mary, "even for plain folk." She hesitated a second, then hunger got the better of her. She snatched a piece of pork from the platter and stuffed it into her mouth.

At that moment John Anderson and Simeon came through the door. Mary started guiltily and quickly turned her back.

"Ha," Simeon jeered. "I wouldn't think a dainty little gal like you would want to eat anything when you spent the whole afternoon in the shit house."

"What's wrong with Henry?" There was panic in John Anderson's deep voice.

Mary told him and showed him what she and Luke had done. By the time she was through explaining, Luke was back with two long, black eels.

"Zeke Bother gave 'em to me. He was out fishing this morning with Jim Morrissay."

Under Mary's instructions, Luke peeled off the eels' skins and wrapped them tightly around Henry's sprains.

"Put the eels in a pot to cook," Mary commanded. "The broth will be good for Henry."

"You're a right smart little gal," said Mr. Anderson gratefully and went to wash himself at the well.

By the time Henry came around half an hour later he was bound and poulticed like a grafted tree. He looked up at Mary's anxious face leaning over him, smiled, and closed his eyes. "I was after a honey-comb for you," he murmured, and would have gone to sleep but Mary insisted on his having a bit of thin gruel first.

"Shall I fetch Miz Whitcomb?" Luke asked his father.

"I guess you're gonna have to."

"I will not be leaving Henry until he is well," Mary declared firmly.

She pulled the rocking-chair over beside Henry's bed and chanted a healing charm for him in Gaelic:

> *Cnèimh ri cnèimh*
> *Cuisil ri cuisil*
> *Céirein ri céirein*
> *Ris a' chois chli.*

Henry woke. "What's them words, miss?

"Healing words, Henry, and I will tell them to you in English, my wee lamb, if you will say my name to me. It is Mairi."

"Mary," mumbled Henry shyly.

She put her hand on his good arm and recited softly:

> Bone to bone
> Vein to vein

Balm to balm
To the left leg
Then to the ankle
And then to the wrist

She got up quietly and brought another dish of cornmeal gruel from the fire and insisted, despite his protests, that Henry eat.

"Good night, Henry."

"Good night, miss—Mary," he whispered. "I like your singing."

All the next day Mary stayed close to him. She would not let him get out of bed. She made him eat more gruel and the eel broth she had cooked for him and she kept everyone else away. His father came once to stand by the foot of the bed, his tall frame sending a shadow along the full length of it.

"You gave us all a bad scare, son," was all he said but it was not difficult to see how relieved he felt— or how tired he was.

Simeon, as much to torment Mary as Henry, shouted at him every time he came into the room, "You all right, Hank?"

"I hate that name," Henry whispered to Mary, but Mary said nothing to Simeon. She knew well the teasing ways of people from her own childhood. How Callum Grant and Johnny Fraser had teased!

Late in the afternoon, exasperated by Mary's protectiveness, Luke pulled her from her chair and propelled her towards the door. "Out!" he thundered, deepening his voice to a low baritone. "You're like a mama cat. I ain't no owl after your kitten. I just want to sit a spell with Henry!"

Mary twisted away from his hand. You…'' she began, but stopped at the smile on his face and went outside. She scrubbed her hands and face at the well, braided her hair and straightened her clothes, then walked across the road to where the cow was browsing by the verge, its calf close beside it. She stroked the cow, knelt by the calf and hugged it. She listened to a pair of goldfinches singing in a willow tree and looked long at the chicory blooming at the edge of the Andersons' dooryard. The comfortable feel of the cow and the calf, the familiar birdsong in the willow, and the blue of the field-flower brought a kind of warmth she had not felt since leaving her own glen. One of the small squirrel-like animals Luke called chipmunks scooted along a fallen tree, a groundhog dove into its hole beside the road. Mary wondered for the first time since she had come to Upper Canada where the unseen creatures dwelt, where the fairy hills were. She went back to her nursing with a lighter heart.

The days settled into a routine. Lydia Anderson stayed in bed. Mary got meals, recalling, if somewhat imperfectly, her days at the Gillespies at Tigh-na-Suidh, and did her best to keep the cabin as neat as Mrs. Whitcomb had left it. She thought about Mrs. Whitcomb's kindness, about the Collivers' kindness, remembered the mean-spiritedness of the man and woman on the road from Cornwall. ''They are not all inhospitable, the folk in Upper Canada,'' she decided. She did not love the work but she had come to care for Henry. She thought he was like a solemn old *bodach* with his big grey eyes in his thin face and his wispy fair hair, and she told him stories and made funny faces to make him laugh. She slept on a blanket on the floor by his bed. She woke nights from troubled dreams, but she never found herself out on the road. She was glad, all the same, that she was not alone.

Luke went to tell Julia Colliver that Mary would be staying for a while and Mrs. Colliver sent her, along with a great deal of advice, a change of clothes and the message that she would be expected back at the Collivers' as soon as Henry was recovered. Mary caught Luke's eye as he was delivering all these messages and saw that he was as amused as she by Mrs. Colliver's overbearing ways.

After a couple of days, Mary allowed Henry to get out of bed, and with her arm and a chair to support him he hopped on his good leg to the table for meals and to the front porch. There he sat, his thin face aglow from the cossetting and the leisure, watching his father and brothers work.

Mrs. Anderson got out of bed when Mrs. Whitcomb came to see how the family was managing. "You need to be firm with Lydia," Mrs. Whitcomb told Mary.

They were sitting with Henry on the porch. His mother was dressing herself in the house. "I can see you're taking good care of everything else." Mrs. Whitcomb smiled. "And I don't even know who you are. I'm Jane Whitcomb and I live down the road a piece, two homesteads on through the bush."

"I am Mary Urquhart, niece to Davie and Jean Cameron who were staying nearby. But they have gone home."

92

"Yes." Mrs. Whitcomb's voice held sympathy. "I knew they had gone but I didn't know you had come. We were so sorry about their son. How that boy could play that wooden flute of his! We used to go up to the head of the bay some summer's evenings just in the hope of hearing him. Jim Morrissay was making him a really fine flute when he…well, I guess he must have been pretty unhappy though you wouldn't have known it from that music. He wasn't around much with the other boys. Kept to himself."

"He was not happy here," Mary said stiffly.

"Alas, there have been many not happy here. These are difficult times for us all. We are refugees and that's not easy for anybody."

"Refugees?"

"When we were children we came up here from the old Thirteen Colonies with our parents—those colonies that are called the United States now. We came up through the woods with little more than the clothes on our backs. Our parents wouldn't fight against the King in the rebellion in '75, so we all had to flee to Canada. We didn't think we had to go to war to let the English government know we didn't like a few laws. The rebels called us traitors— dirty Tories—but we called ourselves Loyalists. We were the ones to stay loyal to the King. We left good, settled homes—my father was a schoolteacher in New York, my husband's father was a preacher in Albany—but that didn't make any difference. Dan Pritchett who's my neighbour now, he came from Staten Island. He was a wheelwright. Like the rest of us, he wasn't for revolution. He went to jail, his wife was left destitute. She died, four of his nine children, too. Dan finally got out of jail. He left New York City with five sons and his sister Sarah. We all came together in the refugee camps at Yamaska near Montreal. We were pretty badly beaten down. Some had been tarred and feathered and ridden out of town on rails by our own neighbours, some had been strung up—hanged like common criminals. My cousin David was and he was only fourteen years old.'' Mrs. Whitcomb looked down at her hands clenched in her lap. ''Then, when we hadn't more than just gotten ourselves settled into these backwoods—not quite thirty years later—didn't those old Yankee neighbours come along and start another war! They thought they'd kick us out of here too. Well, I guess they got a surprise! That war's over now, too—over a year ago and it didn't bother us much down here on the island—though it came close enough. After all, the Americans are just across the lake. Joey Bother was killed at the battle of Chrysler's Farm and we lost Billy Ansel at Sackets Harbour, but we were luckier than many and we had no battles here on the island.''

''Mr. Openshaw took some prisoners,'' Henry said proudly.

''So he did.'' Mrs. Whitcomb chuckled. ''He held them smartly, too, and managed to free a dozen or so of our own boys on account of them. And those Yankees had come ashore—from over at the fort in Oswego, New York, I guess—thinking they were going to take some of us prisoner. Well, all that's finished, now.'' She took Mary's hand and patted it. ''You have come to live among us and I hope you will be happy. It is not such a bad life, in spite of the hardships. We're good enough neighbours. Oh, there you are, Lydia." Mrs. Whitcomb stood up. "There now, I'll make some coffee."

Mrs. Anderson sat down on the step beside Henry. She was shaking, as pale as paper, but she had washed and she had smoothed her hair into a loose knot at the back of her head. She took Henry's hand and, without looking up, she said, "Thank you for taking care of us."

"It was naught but Henry."

"It was baby, too." Mrs. Anderson's voice was barely audible.

"The poor wee thing." Mary couldn't help showing some of the indignation she felt. Mrs. Anderson said no more. Henry wriggled uncomfortably. Mrs. Whitcomb reappeared and they drank their coffee and talked about the harvest to come. Suddenly Simeon came crashing out of the woods from down the road.

"Pritchetts' barn's on fire," he shouted. "Pa and Luke has gone and I'm getting our bucket." He grabbed the bucket from the ledge of the well and charged off down the road.

"Oh, dear." Jane Whitcomb got to her feet. "They'll be needing the women to cook. Do pray the house doesn't catch!" She was off across the yard and down the road after Simeon.

Mary sat glued to the porch. Hot sweat rose from the soles of her feet to the top of her head. "I should have warned them," she thought, "I should have told them."

"Oh, I don't care what Jane Whitcomb says, it's a terrible life." Mrs. Anderson had no thought for the fire. "We lived in a nice town down in the Jerseys. We had a house, a proper house on a proper street with other houses. There were a lot of streets in that town and a square in the middle with a real church on one side where there was a regular preacher. And there was a school with a schoolmaster, and shops—my father kept a store. All he ever wanted was to make a decent living and have peace and quiet and this is what he got—a backwoods full of bears and moose and wolves. I remember us coming up that cussed river and down along the lake on barges like slaves. Well, it killed him and it will kill the rest of us." Shakily she got up and went into the house.

Mary could stand it no longer. She took Henry's hand and peered intently into his startled grey eyes "Don't you go hirpling off *anywhere*, Henry Anderson, or I will put a fine and wicked spell on you," she threatened. She jumped to her feet and tore down the road after Jane Whitcomb and Simeon.

"Oh goodness, Mary, you didn't need to come." Jane Whitcomb was startled when Mary came running up beside her.

"I do." Mary fell into step beside her and together they hurried along the forest road.

"I'm sure we can use another hand. Fires are a terrible threat to us all. Places go up like tinderboxes in the backwoods. Oh dear, I do hope Dan and Martha are all right."

Mary said nothing but silently she prayed fervently that *everybody* would be all right.

The sun sent a shaft of light glinting on the swamp here, illuminating a patch of road there, but the huge trees cast so much shade that it seemed more like late evening than early afternoon. The road led in the opposite direction from the one Luke had taken from the Collivers' to the Anderson homestead so Mary was not prepared for the sight of open water.

They came to a log bridge that spanned a creek leading into a large bay.

"How beautiful!" Mary could not contain her wonder.

"It's Hawthorn Bay," Mrs. Whitcomb told her.

The bay looked to be about three miles long and a quarter of a mile or so wide. It was like a broad neck to a bottle, with the bottle being Lake Ontario at the other end. Mary looked out over the water. She thought she heard music from the reeds along the bay. She wanted desperately to kneel by the creek and put her face in the water, to wade out into it, to walk along its shore out into bright open space. But from where she stood she could see smoke and great orange flames rising above the forest just north of the bay. She began to run.

"We don't need to run," Mrs. Whitcomb called after her.

"I must," Mary cried over her shoulder and raced on—around the end of the bay, along the narrow road, through the deep woods, to the Pritchetts'. She saw flames leaping from the barn, smoke, scurrying figures trying to corral a confusion of screaming horses, squealing pigs, bawling cows and sheep. A double chain of men had formed from the burning building across the yard and down through the trees to the bay. One line was heaving buckets full of water from the bay to the barn, the other was passing the empty buckets back for more water. Several women were herding children towards the bay, away from the fire.

Someone screamed, "Polly! Where's Polly?"

"Oh, my God, she's in the barn! I seen her go in after her kitten and I never seen her...."

Mary did not wait to hear the rest. Flames were pouring out a window on one side of the building, flames were shooting out of the roof at the back, the front doors were open. She dashed into the barn. In the loft a kitten was screaming.

"Polly," she called. "Polly, is you there?"

"Here." It was a small, frightened-sounding voice.

"Where is here, lassie?"

"I'm up in the hayloft—I'm scared," wailed the child.

"Is there a ladder, then?"

"I don't know!"

A sheet of flame raced along the wall beside Mary.

"How did you get up there?"

"I clum up in the back where there's steps but the fire's took them away." Polly began to wail.

"Can you jump?"

"I'm scared."

The fire was coming closer. Polly began to howl, Mary began to cough. She had an inspiration.

"The cat's not scared, Polly. It wants to come down. If you hold tight to the cat, it will see you safe down."

A small blonde head appeared at the edge of the hayloft.

"Come, Polly," said Mary softly. "Puss will help you." She held out her arms. Polly did not move. Her eyes were huge with fear. She leaned farther over the rim of the loft. In her arms she clutched the screaming, wriggling kitten.

The fire crackled. The barn was filling with smoke. There was the odour of burning flesh from somewhere.

"Come, Polly," Mary crooned.

Fire leapt up the side of the loft. Polly backed away from the rim, from the fire. She looked down at Mary. She jumped.

Mary caught her. The cat, with one wild yowl, hurled itself from Polly's arms and out the door. Mary sprinted after it through the door. And collided with Luke. Luke threw his arms around Mary and child, lifted them both, and raced from the barn. There was a crash behind them. The barn roof caved in and the whole structure sank to the ground in a massive bonfire.

Luke did not stop until he was almost at the shore. Almost reluctantly he set them down.

"I thought you'd die in there." His voice was hoarse.

"It was my doing the child was caught. I had to. I...."

"Down," said Polly.

"Och," Mary laughed shakily. She hugged Polly tightly and put her on her feet.

"Polly! Polly! Oh, Polly!" A wild-eyed woman, her hair in disarray, her clothes smudged and torn, was running towards them. Her arms were outstretched.

"Mama!" Mother and child embraced frantically. Mary turned to thank Luke but he had disappeared. She was glad. She did not want to talk to him—or to anybody.

"I did what I came to do," she thought. She looked towards the bay only a few feet away. Swiftly, before anyone could see her leave, she moved up to the shore and along it until she was out of sight of the Pritchett homestead.

CHAPTER VIII
Meadow on the Bay

When she was sure no one had followed, Mary stopped. She breathed in the aroma of fish and waterplants. She felt the breeze. She listened to an oriole singing in a maple tree just back from the marsh. She looked out at the open water, blue and still as glass except for the occasional ripple made by a trout or a pike, a family of ducks, and a pair of black-and-white water-birds diving out in the bay. She gazed until her eyes smarted. Carefully she began to pick her way along the shore.

In some places it was rocky, in some marshy, in some the willow and poplar trees were right at the water's edge and she had to hitch up her skirt, take off her shoes, and wade around them. She came to the end of the trees, to a small meadow, not more than an acre of ground reaching into the bay like a pointing hand. A doe and her fawn were drinking on the far side. At the sound of her, they raised their heads and bounded off.

A few birches, willows, poplars, a number of the hawthorns that had given the bay its name, and a tall tamarack fringed the south-eastern border of the meadow. Otherwise there were no trees, only bushes, tall grass, and wildflowers—milkweed, yarrow, tansy, wild roses—their soft pink and white and yellow colours making a bright pattern, their sweet scents rich on the afternoon air. A creek flowed through the meadow about thirty feet from a log cabin that stood up near the road. A rowan sapling grew by the cabin door.

To ward off evil, Mary knew—and knew too, in that moment, that this had been Uncle Davie's and Aunt Jean's—and Duncan's—house.

"I had not thought to care for a single clod of earth from this dark country, but this...." She revolved slowly on one heel, filling her senses with everything around her. "This is a different place. This is like home." She did not want to go into the cabin—not yet. She went instead to sit on a large, flat, grey rock that reached out over the water where the tip of the meadow touched the bay.

Here she could not see the pebbles or plants through the water's surface as she could along most of the shore and in the creek. It was as though there were a shadow in the water at that spot. "Black water is not good fortune," she murmured. She leaned closer. She heard whistling from along the shore. She looked around. Luke was jumping across the little stream.

For half a second Mary looked blankly at him.

"Hello, Mary."

She stood up, remembering, as though it had happened a long time before, that Luke had run with her and Polly away from the collapsing barn. "Luke Anderson, you saved my life. It was a fine deed and I am grateful to you." The words sounded wrong and stiff in her ears but there did not seem to be any right ones. And, although she had begun to think of Luke as her friend, now she felt awkward and uncomfortable with him, remembering how she had clung to him.

"You saved Polly Pritchett's life." Luke shook his head. "It was a strange wonder, Mary, you running straight into that barn after Polly like that. It seemed almost as if you knew she'd gone in there."

"I did know. I knew it when I got to the wee bridge over the stream. I knew there was to be the fire, too. I knew it the day I locked myself in the privy, the day Henry fell. And I knew he was to fall. You may as well know, Luke," Mary confessed, "I have the two sights."

"What do you mean?"

"The two sights, the *an dà shelladh*. What do *you* say for the seeing into the future and…." Mary stopped. She had suddenly remembered Julia Colliver saying "that nonsense" when she had told her about hearing Duncan call. Now here was Luke facing her with that same uncomprehending gaze.

"It is just the way of it, Luke Anderson," she blurted. "Some folk see into the hind of the world and some do not. And do not you gawp at me so— like a great owl." She stamped her foot in frustration.

"Oh," said Luke. His eyebrows went up but he made no other comment. At last, ignoring her tirade, he said, "I figured I'd find you here."

"This was where Duncan lived." Mary did not have to ask. She could not go on now to say that she had come to Upper Canada because he had called to her. She felt abandoned, forlorn. Duncan was dead, his family had gone home, and there was no one who could understand why she had come to this country.

"I figured maybe he had something to do with it." Luke sounded a bit downhearted.

"Were you friends with Duncan?"

"I don't know as you could say that." Luke hesitated. "He was two or three years younger than me and—and he kept to himself a lot. And he was an up-and-down sort of feller—one day he'd come around laughing and joking and playing on that wooden whistle of his so's it was awful hard not to jump and dance, the next day he was as like to be blacker than all night. He got so there was a sight more black days to him than bright ones. And he was—he had—" Luke hesitated again. "Well, he had a kind of wicked tongue onto him."

"I know that wicked tongue!" Involuntarily the corner of Mary's mouth went up. "He was ever a one to turn that tongue on us at home."

"I guess he wasn't too happy living here."

"He was not. Och, Luke, I can see it now, how he felt suffocated by all these trees!"

"Ain't you got trees in Scotland?"

"There are trees, indeed there are. But all is not forest like this. It is open country—and there are the

hills.'' Mary's face glowed as she described to Luke
what it was like at home. ''It is very different from
here,'' she finished abruptly. ''I must go now to see
to Henry.''

''I expect everybody to Pritchetts' would like to
see you back there. Fire's out. The barn's gone and
they lost four pigs and a cow but Polly's fine. Dan
and Martha was looking for you to tell you their
thanks. I guess they'd like to have you come to the
supper that's being fixed.

''I cannot—Henry—I must go.''

''You don't need to be shy of Dan or Martha or
any of the neighbours. They're kindly enough
folk.''

It was not shyness that kept Mary back, although
she did feel a bit reluctant to face so many strangers.
It was that so much had happened—the fire, Polly,
Luke, finding the meadow and the Camerons'
house.

''It's all right.'' Luke smiled. ''I'll walk along
home with you.''

Together they waded along the shore past the
Pritchetts' to the bridge across the creek. Luke told
Mary that the black-and-white birds she saw play-
ing hide-and-seek out in the bay were loons.

''I have never heard such a sound as the sound of
them!'' It was a high, hollow, laughing sound and
Mary felt sure there was magic in it.

''Them little yellow-and-green birds is called
grassy birds on account of they make their nests in
the grass.'' Luke seemed pleased to be showing
Mary the wonders of his neighbourhood. He
showed her where the red-winged blackbirds

Janet Lunn

rested in the reeds in spring, and where the wild rice grew thick. He showed her the bright orange jewel-weeds that grew in the marsh. "They'll fix you right up if you've broke out with the poison ivy," he said. Then he helped her gather flowers to take home to Henry.

That night, before she went to bed, Mary stood out in the clearing.

"It was wrong of me not to tell what I knew. Though Julia Colliver might say nonsense, the bairn might have died—and her not more than three years old. They had no need to lose the pigs and the cow." She shivered, remembering the odour of burning flesh in the barn. "It might have been Polly and it might have been me. It is true what Mrs. Grant said, I must be what I am, do what I must do. Here is twice, now, I have refused to give warning. First to Luke, then to Dan Pritchett.... Twice? It *is* twice!"

"Twice will you refuse your destiny, twice will you seek it, before you embrace it as your own." She could hear the words in her head as clearly as when Mrs. Grant had pronounced them, standing on the path leading down from the glen. She looked around her at the stump-filled clearing in the forest. She looked up into the night sky. "And the moon is the same moon that watched me leave home that very same night. Och, Mrs. Grant, I will seek my destiny now, once, twice, as many times as I must."

The next day Martha Pritchett came with Polly to see Mary.

"I declare, girl—nothing I can ever do for you can repay you for what you did." She shook Mary's hand. "I've had plenty of occasions to say that child would be the death of me before I've turned forty but I never thought.... Oh, Lord!" Her voice shook and she squeezed Polly so tightly that Polly stopped undoing the buttons on her mother's dress to cry out.

Mary said little. Although she had promised herself, Mrs. Grant, and God in heaven to warn people of the danger she saw for them, she had made up her mind that she would not tell another living soul in this neighbourhood that she had the two sights. She just smiled and assured Martha that she was unhurt.

"Dan would have come along," Martha said, "but he's got too much to do today. He's finding a place for the other three pigs and the cow, and a pen for the sheep, and he's got the boys down clearing for the new barn. You know Dan lost other children back in the war, and he lost his first wife. He's a sight older than I am. Moses Heaton down by the South Bay's my pa. Him and Dan was friends back on Staten Island. Losing the barn is hard but—" She looked down at Polly, who had fallen asleep in her lap.

Mary promised she would go to the barn-raising to meet Dan and his sons and the other children.

The raising was the following week. Because Henry begged so hard, his father said he might go. And because it was more than four miles from the Andersons' to the Pritchetts', John Anderson asked the Whitcombs for a place in their ox-cart for Henry.

By the time they reached the Pritchetts' the barn was well along and trestle tables for dinner had been set up in the yard. Dan Pritchett was a respected and popular man and people had come from over ten miles around to help him raise his new barn—and, of course, for a party. There seemed to Mary to be at least a hundred of them, all wanting to come and cluck over her, shake her hand, marvel over her bravery, and tell her how sorry they felt about her aunt and uncle leaving with their boys.

They began even before she had got Henry settled under the big maple tree near where the carts were gathered.

"Welcome to our little community, you brave gal! My name's Hannah Foster and I live down to Partridge Hollow. You'll be a welcome sight in my front room any time you care to come by!" The stout old woman grabbed Mary's hand and shook it vigorously.

"Now then, Hannah, don't hog the girl. So you're Mary Urkit, are you? Well, well! Not much of you to be so brave, is there? And I hear you been right smart with young Henry Anderson. Looks like them Andersons struck it lucky."

"Lucky is right!" It was Julia Colliver. "But she'll be back with us before long, Betsy Armstrong. Well, Mary, I guess you been making quite a name for yourself, ain't you? I'm right proud of you." Mrs. Colliver beamed as though Mary were her cow that had just won first prize at the fair.

"Thank you," was all Mary managed to say to Mrs. Colliver before there was another. "So here's the little gal who came along too late to find her family and just in time to save little Polly Pritchett.

Well, we'll all have to be your family now." It was a kindly old woman Mrs. Colliver introduced as Charlotte Heaton. Then came Phoebe Morrissay who put her arms around her and told her she was "blessed if ever there were blessed folk" and others named Bother, Yardley, O'Casey, Schneider. There was a sour old lady who told her she was sure that she'd "come along, a perfect stranger, to take the good husbands away from our fine girls."

Patty Openshaw came charging through the crowd in her bright blue clothes. "There you are," she cried happily. "I was hoping you'd come along. Come on, leave Henry be a minute." She grabbed Mary by the hand and pulled her over to the lunch tables. "I got to stand here and keep the flies away when Ma and the rest sets out the food. You can keep me company. Do you figure on marrying Luke Anderson?"

Mary's mouth fell open.

"Do you?"

"I…I…. Where did you get such a notion?"

"Ain't you interested in marrying Luke?"

Mary blushed, deeply embarrassed for this outspoken girl.

"You are." Patty's face fell.

"I am not. I am not interested in marrying Luke. I am not interested in marrying anybody."

"Cross your heart?"

"Och, indeed, I…."

"Then you got no objection to me setting my cap for him?"

"Does he like blue?" Mary was beginning to be more amused than horrified.

"Huh? Oh, well, it's my ma, not me." Patty laughed, looking down at her dress. "Pedlar sold her a whole bolt. Come on, let's go on over and watch the men, the flies will keep!"

Mary did not want to watch the men. She had had enough of the women, too. They had all been kind, but she was not used to large gatherings and, what's more, she had really come to the barn-raising so that she could go along the bay to her meadow. She glanced at Henry. He was showing off his sprains and breaks to an admiring audience of small children.

"I will come soon," Mary told Patty. She headed through the crowd towards the bay. Paying no attention to anyone, she all but bumped into a little, grey-bonneted, grey-gowned woman going in the opposite direction, her head lowered, her hands folded.

"Oh, I'm terribly sorry." The little grey woman gasped. "I didn't see, I mean I didn't…oh, I'm sorry." She reminded Mary so much of a timid old ewe that she almost patted her back reassuringly. In an effort to stifle a giggle she introduced herself.

"Oh, I am pleased to meet you. I am Sarah Pritchett, sister to Dan Pritchett. We are so grateful to you, Mary. You have been our angel of mercy. We will never forget…oh, dear, there's Martha looking for me. Excuse me, I'd better…oh, dear!" Sarah scuttled off nervously towards the house.

Mary flew across the yard and through the thin line of trees to the shore. She hurried along the edge of the water, not stopping until she reached the meadow, her meadow, Duncan's meadow.

She intended to go into the house but, somehow, she found herself kneeling on the big, grey rock out on the point. There was something about that dark water that drew her. She leaned into it until her face was almost touching it. She had almost lost her balance when a small sound made her aware that she was being watched. She leapt up and whirled around. A dark-skinned woman was standing by the stream up near the cabin looking intently at her.

The woman was small and round—round-bodied, round-faced. She was dressed in deerskin leggings and her knee-length leather shift was decorated with tiny many-coloured beads and fringed at the bottom. On her feet she wore soft leather moccasins, also fringed. Her shining black hair hung down her back in two long braids. Mary realized that she was an Indian and remembered her terrifying encounter with the man in the swamp on her way from Cornwall. This time she had no wish to flee. The woman did not smile but her face was kind. "Owena," she pointed to herself.

"Mairi," Mary pointed to herself and walked across the grass.

"I come for the mint Jean planted. It is for tea. There are good herbs here on the island." Mary said nothing for a moment. She was thinking of the other half of what she had to learn in order to fulfil the destiny Mrs. Grant had said was hers. A healer, Mrs. Grant had said, and it was time. She thought of Henry's accident and how she had needed to care for him. Maybe Owena would teach her about these herbs.

"You will teach me?" Owena inclined her head. She stooped and began to pick the tall mint growing along the verge of the creek. Mary turned her attention to the cabin. She paused by the little rowan tree and touched its bark affectionately.

The cabin was about the same size as the Andersons'. It had a bark roof, no front porch, one glazed window, and a plank door. There was a garden in front, overgrown with ripe melons and squash. Mary paused at the door. She asked the house's permission to enter, lifted the latch string, pushed open the door, and went inside.

It was as though Aunt Jean and Uncle Davie, Callum and Iain had only just left, but that the fire had gone cold on the hearth. A black squirrel scampered into the rafters and a mouse scurried across the room to hide in the log wall. Except for a bit of chewed-up rag and small animal droppings near the cupboard, it was tidy—so unlike the Andersons' squalid place. Otherwise it was much the same: the large fireplace and chimney against the back wall, a tall dresser at right angles to it along one side wall, the bed built into the back corner, the square pine table in the centre of the room, a rocking-chair and a three-legged stool by the fireplace. Beside the front door was the glass window and coming halfway across the room was an open loft with a ladder leading to it.

In the loft were three more wooden bedframes. Aunt Jean would have taken the bedding with her and thrown out the straw, Mary knew. There was a little triangular window-opening from which she could see out over the bay. "How Callum and wee Iain must have liked this window," she thought, then realized with shock that she hadn't thought of Duncan looking through the window, hadn't thought of Duncan at all, in the loft or downstairs.

"He is not here. He is nowhere in the house." She had felt Aunt Jean's presence so powerfully in the way the house was kept, in her rocking-chair by the hearth. She had felt Uncle Davie in the painstakingly fashioned dresser, the table, stool, and benches. Callum and Iain were there too, sitting by the fire, at the table, and upstairs, "But you are not here, Duncan. I cannot find you here!"

She went back outside. Owena had gone. She went around behind the house and across the road to a clearing in the pine forest where there were chokecherry and hawthorn trees and a small barn. Behind it was a single grave marked by a crudely squared granite boulder with the words chipped into it.

DUNCAN GRANT CAMERON

BORN 2 MAY 1800

GLEN URQUHART SCOTLAND

DIED 10 JUNE 1815

HAWTHORN BAY UPPER CANADA

She sat down and slowly ran her fingers over each letter, each number, hoping desperately to bring Duncan's presence to her.

"You called me! You were thousands of miles from home and when I came you were gone. The tenth of June. I was on my way! Here am I now and I cannot reach you, I cannot find your spirit." She grasped the sides of the gravestone and put her head down on its rim.

"When I see so much," she cried in grief as she had once done in rage, "so much that I do not wish

113

of others' lives, why can I not see this that matters so much to me?'' She shook her fist up at the dark trees. "You have stolen him from me. You have swallowed him whole. Give him back!'' She stayed there a long time, tracing Duncan's name over and over, then, when the shadows of the giant trees were long across the meadow, she went to stand once more on the large grey rock and peer into the dark water.

Again she was interrupted, this time by the sound of someone running down the road. It was Luke. He came across the grass towards her. "I knew I would find you here.''

At once Mary became alarmed. "Henry? Has something happened to Henry?''

"Henry's all right. He.... I didn't come to talk about Henry. Mary, why did you come here again?''

"I mean to come here to live.'' As she said the words she knew she meant them. "I do. I mean to come here to live.''

"Why? It's not good here.''

At first Mary made no reply. "There are no trees,'' she said, finally. It was all she was willing to say.

"No people, neither.'' Luke wandered over to the stream where Owena had stood earlier, bent down and picked up a pebble, stood up, tossed the pebble back and forth from one hand to the other. "Mary, I....''

Mary remembered the conversation she had had with Patty Openshaw, knew what he was going to say, and desperately did not want him to say it.

"Mary, I'd like for you to marry me.'' His words rushed forward as if bent on getting said before she

114

could stop them. "I didn't mean to speak so soon. I know what a bad time it's been for you, but it ain't going to help for you to come to live in this place. You'd be here all alone. Before you come along I never thought to git married. But I'm nineteen years old with a bit of money saved for a piece of land. I ain't one bit like Duncan Cameron with his good-looking face and his fine fluting that could get us all laughing and crying, but I cut a fine reel on the dance floor and—well, the cows like me well enough and I'm mighty well thought of in the barn yard at feeding time," he grinned, "and...well, I wish you would marry me, Mary."

Mary almost said, "Marry Patty Openshaw—she wants to," but she stopped herself. "Luke, you do not know me!" She managed a steady voice though she did not feel a bit steady.

"I guess you could say that, but I sort of feel as if I do. The first time I set eyes on you, back when you was walking from Soames to the Corners, I looked at you with your black hair all shiny around your white face, and your black eyes, and, Mary, I just figured you was the one I was going to marry."

"Luke, it cannot be. I will not, I cannot marry— ever."

"I guess I didn't pick much of a time to be asking, but...well, I'd be afraid for you living here, Mary. Come home and stay with us. I won't pester you about marrying, won't bring the subject up again. But don't stay here!"

"But I mean to live here, Luke. Henry is mending. He does not need me now. I must come home with you now, for I will not leave your mother or

Henry without a word, but I will come here to live in this place until I have earned my passage home. You must not speak to me again about marrying, for I will not.''

Luke did not move at once. His eyes travelled from Mary's face to the house, to the water, across the road and back again. ''Come on,'' he said. ''Let's fetch Henry and take him on home.''

CHAPTER IX

The House at
Hawthorn Bay

The Camerons' house belonged to Dan Pritchett now, Luke told Mary. So she went to see Dan the next morning. She found him in the new barn, constructing stalls for his livestock.

"Sure you can live there if you want. I'm glad to be able to do something for you, Mistress Mary," Dan boomed. He was a huge, bluff man. "Three axe handles across the shoulders," as Luke described him, and at least a head and a half taller than either Luke or his father.

He was glad to have Mary in the house. "Nobody here needs that house just now. Davie and Jean Cameron bought it from Charity Hazen. She and her husband Zeke were Vermont Loyalists and he got so homesick for his hills he took a chance on being imprisoned or done to death, and he went back home—never been heard from again. When the Camerons wanted to sell I was glad to get another hundred acres, but it's gonna be a snowy Sunday in July before we get to clearing that piece of land. It's a bit far from the barn to be tethering a cow and—well, as you know, we're short a cow now anyways.''

Mary asked if she might tend his sheep for the rent. ''Now, now,'' he said, ''Martha and I, we're right glad to be doing a good turn to the gal who saved our Polly. Don't you think on it.'' So Mary thanked him and asked if she could tend the sheep for money.

''Well, my girl,'' he said, ''it's like this; we don't let our sheep roam far enough to need tending, there's too many wolves prowling around the woods. It's only a couple of years or so we've been keeping sheep at all.'' He rubbed his hand across his bald head. Then he wrinkled up his face in thought. ''Can you read?'' he asked.

''I can.''

''Well then,'' Dan beamed. ''I have just the thing. My sister Sarah teaches some of the young ones hereabouts—girls and boys—to read and cipher, as we ain't got any real kind of a school going yet. Now Sarah's a mighty fine woman, but she sometimes has a speck of trouble keeping those older boys reined in. In consequence they don't get too much learning into 'em.''

Mary thought of little grey Sarah Pritchett scurrying at the sound of her sister-in-law's voice. ''I am not afraid of the children,'' she said.

''Do you think they could hear a word you said to 'em?'' Dan slapped his leg and roared with laughter. ''You people from Scotland, you talk so a fellow has to strain his ears, even big ones like mine, just to catch a word. A pretty sound, mind you," he added.

"It is all the better, then," replied Mary tartly. "The great lads will need to be still to catch the sound of the pretty words."

Dan laughed again. "You'll be all right. And Martha will sure be glad to get that babble and shouting out of our house, and Sarah will be mighty pleased to have the help! I'll throw in your winter's supply of firewood and a share of the flour and potatoes that come our way from the neighbours whose kids is coming to Sarah's school."

A winter's supply of wood plus food. How much faster she could save what she might earn from Julia Colliver! "How many days a week would the teaching be?" she demanded.

"Well, Sarah generally runs to five mornings a week. The folks needs their children to work in the afternoons and, mind you, the older children won't come until after the harvest is in, anyways."

"I will do it," decided Mary.

"Suppose we go tell Martha and see if she don't rustle us up a saucer of tea and something to eat." Dan led the way out of the barn.

After half an hour with Dan, Martha, and Polly, who came to sit on her lap and show her the doll Charlotte Heaton had made for her, Mary went to see Julia Colliver about working afternoons in payment for wool and the weaving lessons she had once offered. She meant to do as Mrs. Colliver had suggested—weave for her passage home.

"Mary, you can't live there!" Mrs. Colliver was scandalized. "You come here to us. You can have

Janet Lunn

that room behind the stairs all to yourself. What's the matter with you! A young girl like you thinking of living alone? I don't know what it's like back in your country but we don't do things like that here. Why, think of the dangers. Wild animals. In the winter when it gets cold, the wolves come right up to the door. And bears. And there's Indians. I happen to know there's been Indians coming and going from that house regular since it's been empty. Jean was foolish, she used to let them come, and since the house has been empty, they been squatting there by times."

"I have met an Indian woman. I liked her."

"Well, you might not like it when the whole tribe moves in on you. These Indians, you don't know them, they're Mohawks. Us Yorkers from near Troy knew them back home. They was as like to take your scalp and set fire to your house as look at you. You can't trust those people."

Mrs. Colliver paused. Mary said nothing.

"It ain't just Indians. A young girl like you alone with no husband—it ain't to be considered. What's more, young woman, do you know how cold it gets around here in winter? I heard your Aunt Jean say, more than once, if she'd a knew how cold it was going to be in Canada she might not have come here." Mrs. Colliver paused for breath.

"Dan Pritchett will be giving me firewood for the winter."

"Is that so?" Mrs. Colliver was a bit taken aback.

"I will be teaching the school with Sarah Pritchett."

"Can you read?"

120

"I can."

"Hmph. Well, you sure have it all set up, haven't you?"

Mary said softly, "I hope so. Surely I hope so."

It was agreed that she would work for Mrs. Colliver every afternoon in exchange for a small wage, a hank of spun wool to begin weaving with, and a share of the autumn shearing. Anxious to settle herself, Mary hurried to get her things from the Andersons'.

Lydia Anderson wrung her hands. "Oh dear. I thought you might stay here with us. Henry's leg and...the cooking...Luke...I need you." She looked helplessly at Mary.

"I am sorry, Mrs. Anderson." In spite of herself, Mary had become, if not actually fond, protective of Lydia Anderson. "The sweetest, gentlest, prettiest girl in the Midland district, she was," Mrs. Colliver had said. "John was besotted over her." The shadow of the pretty girl was there yet in the drawn, lined face, and although the gentleness had degenerated into unhappy complaint the sweetness was still evident in her childlike concern about Henry, and the wistful way she sometimes looked at her older sons.

Mary was tempted for a moment to change her mind but she did not. "Henry is truly mending, Mrs. Anderson. He does not need me and...." She looked up to see Luke standing in the doorway. She leapt from her chair as though stung, acutely self-conscious.

"And I will come to see you...and to see Henry. Please tell Mr. Anderson and Simeon goodbye for me."

121

"Oh, dear." Lydia Anderson wrung her hands again, her brow furrowed, and Mary knew that as soon as she had gone through the door she would sit down in the rocking-chair and begin to drink from the jug. She had a fleeting vision of Lydia Anderson struggling against wild wind and snow. "I could not save her from it did I stay," she thought defensively, but remembering her vow she put her hand on Mrs. Anderson's arm and looked at her intently. "Please, Mrs. Anderson, when winter comes do not you go out into the snow." She turned to leave, glancing at Luke and away again.

"Goodbye, Mary...." Luke did not seem in the least ill at ease. "Henry and me'll come by to see you when he can get that far on his leg."

"Goodbye." She hurried past him.

Outside she sat beside Henry and told him she was leaving. "I will come to see you," she promised.

Henry's lower lip quivered. His eyes filled with tears. "I don't want you to go." He sniffed.

"Tell Simeon that if he is hard on you I will put a fine spell on him," she whispered, "and he will wither and die as did the poor lad the witch hated in the tale I told you. Remember?"

Henry nodded vigorously, but he did not smile. Mary wished she could take him with her.

By the time she reached her house it was evening and the sun, an enormous glowing scarlet ball, was setting over the woods, casting a wide pink reflection over the bay. The crickets were cricking and the frogs were garumphing in the marsh and the great blue herons were gronking hoarsely as they settled for the night in the branches of the oak and elm trees. A raccoon and her young were washing fish at the mouth of the creek; out on the bay the loons swimming along the surface of the water made ripples and small splashes, calling to one another in their high, hollow tremolos.

Hugging her bundle of belongings tightly to her, Mary surveyed her small kingdom joyfully. Before she entered the house she asked God's blessing. Inside, she found that someone had put a badly darned but serviceable mattress ticking filled with fresh bedstraw in the bed in the corner. There was a loaf of bread on the table. In the cupboard, besides the five wooden trenchers the Cameron family had left behind, were a tin cup and a blue crockery bowl with only a small chunk chipped out of it. The fire was laid and over it hung a much-mended iron open kettle still sound enough to hold water.

Mary was stupefied. The bundle of clothes fell to the floor as she gazed about her.

"It is the *sitheachean*," she whispered. "The fairies wish me well. The old ones are looking after me. If Luke and Mrs. Colliver do not understand those of us with the two sights, they cannot gainsay the old ones! I will be well in Duncan's house with the fairies looking after me." She hung her two shawls, her spare skirt, and a petticoat Mrs. Colliver had given her on the pine-wood pegs by the door and placed her shoes on the floor beneath. She took Mrs. Grant's much-smudged, folded, worn letter from the pocket of her skirt and put it on the top shelf of the dresser. She held the spindle whorl for a moment in her hand.

"You *are* my good fortune. I know it now. It is right what I am doing." She set the spindle whorl beside the letter. Then she picked up the blue crockery dish, carried it outside to the stream, and filled it with water. She walked three times around the house clockwise—very slowly—sprinkling the water and chanting the house-blessing that had always been used in the glen. She filled the little bowl once more and set it by the door.

"I have no milk for you, *bodach*," she addressed the house spirit, although she could not see him, "but I will get you bread and soon I will find milk." She got up and went to stand again in the middle of her meadow. She felt the cool evening breeze and sniffed the sweet milkweed and the cinnamon scent of the rose hips. Then, unmindful of the tall grass, she lifted her skirts to her knees, held her elbows wide, and began to dance. Around and around she danced, faster and faster, her small white feet leaping high, her long black hair flying wild.

Suddenly she stopped. She froze with one foot on the big grey rock at the edge of the water. After a moment her arms fell to her sides. She stared into the bog-black water lapping against the shore. A chill ran through her and she fled to the house. Her elation was gone. In its place was an uneasiness she could not identify.

That night she woke again from the nightmare of Duncan calling her. She found herself crouched half-way across the room, wakened because she had stumbled on something. It was the spindle whorl. She sat down in Aunt Jean's rocking chair by the smouldering fire, twisting the spindle whorl around and around in her hands, wondering how it had come there, wondering where she had been going when she had stumbled over it.

CHAPTER X
The Old Ones Are Looking After Me

"An evil spirit is sending me the dream. It has taken Duncan. It has taken Duncan's voice and now it comes for me." Mary had been badly frightened in the night. "But the old ones are looking after me—I will come to no harm."

All the same, she took a red thread from her petticoat and tied it around her wrist, and she went every morning to Duncan's grave to say a prayer for the return of his spirit so that it might rest. Feeling secure with these protections against the evil, she began life in her new home.

She asked for a bit of paper from Julia as her first week's wages, and wrote to her mother and father. She told them, in as many words as the small paper would allow, what she had been doing, that she was well and that, God willing, she would return to them in the spring—although the mere thought of facing the trip home made her shudder and her stomach contract. She signed the letter "your loving daughter" and took it to Mrs. Hazen at the store to send to Soames to go out on the next ship down the lake.

Next she took stock of what she had and what she had to do. She was determined to prove to Julia Colliver that she could manage by herself. Housekeeping was not as unpleasant as Mary had once thought it would be. Water for cooking and washing flowed in the stream that meandered through her yard. True to his word, Dan Pritchett had seen to it there was wood piled against the side of her house, and she soon learned how to manage a wood fire. Cooking, she had discovered while at the Andersons', was not something she liked doing, but food was plentiful—Dan had brought her a peck of potatoes, there were the squash and pumpkins in what had been Aunt Jean's garden. There were wild greens and the bay was full of fish. Now and then Julia gave her a pitcher of milk or a bowl of butter. Patty Openshaw came up the road one afternoon with a crockery pot, steam rising from under a crust that covered it, and an old blue-and-white checked blanket. "I got to run," she said breathlessly, "Ma's in a tizzy over Aaron on account of he et a grasshopper—here's a pigeon pie and Ma says you can have the coverlet. If she'll let me out by myself for five minutes, I'll come along and we'll have a chin-wag. I only live a mile and a half up the road." Patty deposited the pot into Mary's hands, the blanket on the table, and ran off. "You can keep the pot," she shouted as she went. "Ma says it's for welcome." Once in a while there was a pigeon's breast, a fish, a grouse, or a partridge, plucked and cleaned, sitting on her table when she came in from work in the evening. She knew she was being cared for. "Where, in such low, tree-covered country, do the old ones stay?" she would ask herself.

She loved her meadow and the bay. Often she rose early, wakened by the loons' cries, to watch them play together, diving down into the water, gliding along the surface, disappearing into the mist. She would walk slowly around the entire acre of land, startling the birds and the orange-and-black monarch butterflies into sudden flight, surprising the squirrels and chipmunks so that they scurried up into the trees where they flicked their tails and scolded volubly. They made her laugh.

She never went near the big grey rock down where the meadow pointed into the bay. Sometimes, as she washed her clothes in the stream, gathered mint and tansy for her tea, or collected other herbs for her lessons with Owena, she would look towards it. "There is something evil in that place," and she would think gratefully of her protectors.

Owena had come again the day after Mary moved into her house. "I will teach you," she said. "You have the healing hands. I, too." Mary already knew that. Owena had brought plants from the forest. Together she and Mary collected herbs from along the road and the bay, from Mary's own meadow, and from around the edge of the clearing across the road behind the little barn.

"This one, thistle, is no good for anything."
Owena threw it out. "Basil will discourage flies
from the house." She hung it over the fireplace.
"Feverfew is good for toothache and for fever.
Garlic, too. Yarrow has good smell and makes tea
for chills. Rose hips are for tea to keep off scurvy.
Wild yam is for seizure, sumac for gargling. Be careful of what you call Indian turnip when it is fresh—
it burns. Cook it, then it is good for babies with the
belly-ache. It is good, too, for the coughing
sickness."

Mary found that she remembered more names,
more cures from Mrs. Grant's teaching than she had
any idea she had ever learned. Some plants were
new to her: yams, sumac, crowfoot—not to drink
or eat, good for bad rash on the skin, Owena said.
Others—hyssop, tansy, rose, sage, mint—were so
familiar she could imagine that she was back in Mrs.
Grant's garden under the brow of Drum Eildean.
She was sure Mrs. Grant would like Owena. Owena
spoke in few and quiet words. She was a good
teacher, endlessly patient and thorough.

Sometimes Owena came just to visit, alone or
with friends and relatives, Mohawks who had been
used to visiting Aunt Jean and Uncle Davie. Mary
liked them. She liked the silent, companionable
way they came and went, although it sometimes
startled her. She liked the deep, guttural sound of
their speech, even though she couldn't understand
the words, and she loved to hear them sing. Their
singing was not so different from some she knew
from home. In other ways, too, she sometimes felt
easier with the Indians than she did with her white

neighbours. They read the wind and respected the spirits and creatures of the other world and the ghosts of the dead. But they were also forest people, who would leave her house and disappear into the trees, a barrier too great for Mary to breach.

When Patty Openshaw could steal the time from home she would come galloping up the road through the woods, bonnet strings flapping, to share a five-minute visit in the sun.

Neighbours invited her to "come along to supper." Some weeks, on Saturday or Sunday, Dan Pritchett had prayers and Bible readings in his front room, as there was no church in the community yet and the preacher did not reach them more than once or twice a year.

Mary went every afternoon to her job at the Collivers'. She did not like scrubbing floors or washing dishes, or labouring at all the household chores she had refused to give her life to, at the age of eleven, for Mr. and Mrs. Gillespie.

"Could I have but known," she lamented bitterly as she pared potatoes, or wept as she sliced onions. "Duncan *dubh*, for your sake I came to this wilderness to spend my days as a scullerymaid!"

The outside work was good. When it was shearing time, Mary sang shearing songs to the sheep and taught the words to Matthew and Deborah and Nancy Colliver.

"I declare"—Mrs. Colliver was astonished—"I never in my life saw sheep come like that to nobody. A body could almost believe in magic."

"It is not magic. I know how to talk to beasts," said Mary simply.

131

Some evenings she stayed on to help with supper so that she could weave with Mrs. Colliver afterwards. The work was frustratingly slow; Mary had no patience for it and she could hardly bear Mrs. Colliver's unceasing talk, cheerful as it was. "It is awful work to have to do for an awful journey to have to make," she thought grimly as she wove—and then unwove all her mistakes. But she did not give up. She needed the money her weaving would bring. The hired work she did for the Collivers did little more than pay for her needs.

The spinning at home was no easier. Mary worked on old Mrs. Grant's spindle whorl, slowly and painfully pulling the thread through the hole. Many an evening she balled the split, broken, or tangled wool and almost pitched it into the fire. Then Mrs. Grant's face would appear to her and she would hear again her gently reproving words, "Mairi, Mairi, the good Lord gave patience to us all. Yours is like the wild honey, sweeter and more precious for being long to seek and tormenting to secure."

"Tormenting it is! Tormenting! Tormenting! I shall never make a fine, smooth thread, never!" She would hurl the spindle whorl across the room—but after a while she would retrieve it and begin again. And in time she had threads she felt her mother might not scorn.

But what made it so much harder was that, awake or asleep, she would suddenly hear Duncan cajoling, pleading with her to come to him. She felt the evil spirit was mocking her with Duncan's voice, and then she would cling to Mrs. Grant's spindle whorl for her salvation.

Autumn came and school began. Mary was to teach the reading, Sarah Pritchett the arithmetic. Dan Pritchett had sent a round-up of his grandsons with three long benches to fill up Mary's house. Sarah came in a neat gown and old-fashioned hat, apologizing for taking up all Mary's room, bearing an assortment of hornbooks and primers. Hornbooks Mary had not seen before—they were small, oblong, wooden paddles with an alphabet and a few biblical verses on paper covered by a thin sheet of horn tacked to one side. The primers, tattered as they were, many with pages missing, were more useful. "But they are so old," sighed Sarah. "Mere remnants of the books and hornbooks the children's parents and grandparents learned from in grammar schools back home in the Thirteen Colonies before the rebellion. Well, we must do the best we can." She sighed again.

The children—eleven of them—ranged in age from six to nine. And sometimes Polly Pritchett came too because she put up such a howl of rage at being refused. They came shyly at first, but before long the boys of eight and nine were doing their best to reduce their new reading teacher to the tears to which Sarah Pritchett so easily succumbed.

Mary had not spent fifteen years fighting off foxes, wolves, and the troublesome spirits of the hills to keep her sheep and cattle safe, just to be destroyed by a handful of mischievous boys. When Ben Bother began to croak like a bullfrog while Abe Morrissay was stumbling through his lesson, Mary interrupted Abe. Without raising her voice, she told the tale of the unfortunate Highland boy who had

133

once baa-ed like a sheep in school to confuse the dominie and had had to spend the rest of his eighty-seven years as a sheep.

"Folk took to going out into the meadow just to keep the poor lad company but he would only look skintwise at them with his great, sad eyes, then turn away his head, so ashamed was he of the shape he had taken."

There were a few sniggers and the children all looked at each other disbelievingly, but Ben stopped the bullfrog sounds. Whatever trick the boys were up to, although she might long to fling their precious books at them, Mary would reprimand in even tones or tell a wicked story. And she had a way of narrowing her black eyes and intoning low, slow rhymes in Gaelic that sometimes amused them but as often froze a culprit in his seat to the delight of the others.

Sarah was grateful for the discipline but worried about the effect of the rhymes. She taxed Mary with them one day after school was out.

"I would not repeat real spells!" Mary was indignant. "I only tell them silly rhymes."

"What do you mean, Mary, real spells?"

"*Iùilas*, runes, charms. Spells."

"But you don't really believe in spells? I mean, only the superstitious believe in spells. Oh dear, I...." Sarah fidgeted with the sash of her dress.

Mary didn't know what to say. Here it was again: Mrs. Colliver saying talk of ghosts was nonsense, Luke carefully ignoring what she said about having the two sights, now Sarah Pritchett's "But you don't really believe in spells?" What was wrong with the folk in this country? She opened her mouth to ask Sarah what made them all so foolish but Sarah looked so small—although she was taller than Mary herself—and she was twisting her good silk sash so nervously that Mary could only repeat lamely, "Och, it is but silly rhymes I am giving them." She promised not to frighten the children any more.

There were some evenings when she was grateful to all the spirits of that world in which Sarah Pritchett did not believe. While she spun, the cold autumn wind whistled and wailed through every chink in the little log house, and always it implored her in Duncan's own voice, "Mairi, Mairi, come to me. Mairi!"

She had taken to barricading her door from within so that she could not follow the cry in her sleep, and on some nights only her conviction that the fairies were looking after her kept her from running to the Collivers or the Andersons for safety.

The air was clear, the October sky a cornflower blue; the mosquitoes had disappeared and the flies bothered only during the hottest time of day. The summer birds had all gone south, the little chickadees fluttered about cheerfully, ignoring the noisy jays and the woodpeckers. Occasionally a scarlet cardinal could be seen in the cedars or near the berry bushes.

Frost had struck the forest and the maples had turned tawny, saffron, and scarlet. The oaks were a rich, leathery brown and the birches and hawthorns deep gold. Woven into all this flamboyant colour were the dark evergreens. On the fringe of the woods and along fences the sumac bushes rose like crimson fountains above the thick clusters of purple and white Michaelmas daisies. Mary had never seen such riotous colour in her life and she was so captivated by it that she actually looked forward to her walks through the trees to Collivers' Corners.

It was almost easy to forget her fear in such an atmosphere, and Mary threw herself eagerly into Mrs. Colliver's autumn work. There were still chokecherries, rose hips, and partridgeberries to be made into jams and conserves. The root vegetables had to be dug and stored in the cellars hollowed out of the ground for them. Onions and cucumbers had to be pickled, beans dried. Late-blooming dye plants had to be boiled, then the flax and wool dyed. Pork had to be salted, and the rabbits and the wings and breasts of the passenger pigeons to be jugged.

"It is like making ready for a siege," said Mary.

"Well, I guess you might call winter that." Mrs. Colliver slapped a side of bacon onto the table. "I was about half your age when the rebellion began in '75. We lived near Troy in New York and I mind well sieges and starvation. I don't mean to go hungry nor see any of my family go hungry through war or winter. Now let's get them pritters and turnips dug and into the root cellar."

Mary liked best the days Patty Openshaw came to help. Patty's friendliness and her effervescence could make her forget that she was far from home among alien people.

One day Patty was stirring dye in the big iron pot that had been brought out to hang over the tripod in the back yard while Mary draped the freshly dyed hanks of wool and flax over the fence.

"Say, Mary, don't you get awful lonely living in your auntie's house by yourself? Don't you wish you was back to Andersons'? I mean, there's Luke."

"I do not."

"Ain't you a funny one? You come all this way alone and now you're setting up by yourself in that house. Don't you *really* want to get married? You'll be an old woman and still be there by yourself. You're little but I'll bet you're as old as me—I'm fifteen and I figure if I wait much longer I'll be an old maid."

Temper flared in Mary, hot and sudden. "Am I so very funny?" she cried. "Am I more funny than Julia Colliver or Sarah Pritchett or you who bounce around like a great, blue hen shouting out every word that comes into your head, telling all the world that is not like yourself that it is funny? I am not funny! I came here by myself because... because I had good reason. But I will not stay. And I do not mean to marry. Go you yourself to work for Lydia Anderson—the dear Lord knows she needs help—and marry Luke. Go now, this very afternoon, this very moment." She picked up a dripping hank of red wool and began to wring it savagely.

"Oh!" Patty dropped the stir stick, spattering sumac juice far and wide. "Oh, Mary, I didn't mean to say you was funny *that* way. I just meant...oh, it's true, I never know when to shut my mouth. Oh, what can I say, I feel so bad!" Patty's face was nearly as crimson as the sumac in the pot, her bright blonde hair had come undone from its knot and fell untidily down her back, the dye had spotted her face even more liberally than her cap or apron. As the blush faded she looked like someone with measles. In spite of herself, Mary began to laugh.

Patty's face brightened. She skipped across the yard and threw her arms around her.

Uncomfortably Mary pulled away. She straightened her clothes.

"I like you," said Patty. "I like the way you laugh sort of like one of them woodbirds, up and down, up and down. I never heard you laugh before but, landsakes, you do have a sharp tongue!"

"Girls!" Mrs. Colliver's voice was sharp. "It's growing late. You're both gonna be here in the cold and dark stirring sumac juice and wringing out yarn if you don't busy yourselves."

"Yes ma'am!" Patty began to stir vigorously. Mary picked the dripping wool from the ground and put it over the fence. She didn't know how to react to such affection, nor why she had so lost her temper. She was ashamed of herself.

Later the two walked home together. When Mary stopped at her own home, she put out her hand. She knew she had been unfriendly.

"I am not so very lonely, Patty," she said, "but I should like you to come for a wee visit of an evening." In a burst of confidence, she added, "I am well in my house, I am protected against the evil by the fairies. They brought me gifts of a fine mattress cover and a loaf of bread and a bit of crockery when I came here." She stopped. "Why do you look at me in that way?"

Patty shrugged. She looked embarrassed. "I don't know about fairies, but I know who brought all that stuff. Luke Anderson was by our house after a mattress cover. I think he got one across to Morrissays', and maybe they had a crock too. He was mighty keen, I figure, on getting you made comfortable."

Mary turned cold. She stared at Patty a moment, then ran down the slope to her house. She heard Patty call after her but she did not answer. She ran inside the cabin and slammed the door after her. Leaning against it, her heart beating as though she had run for miles, she stared at the benches, the table, the embers in the fireplace, as though she had never seen them there before. Everything looked strange, unprotected.

"It was not the fairies at all. It was Luke. It was Luke." It was all she could think. Luke had brought the mattress, the crockery, the bread. Luke had been bringing the fish and the birds. "How can I have been so daft?" she thought. "Fairy gifts are not like this. Fairy gifts are not ordinary things like these. How *could* I have been so daft?"

Then she had another—worse—thought. "What if there are no fairies in this place? What if there is nothing protecting me at all from the evil spirit that comes for me? Dear Lord, what am I to do?"

CHAPTER XI
Henry

All the next afternoon, while she peeled and strung apples and helped to hang them from the rafters in Julia Colliver's kitchen, Mary chattered so feverishly that Mrs. Colliver asked her suspiciously if she had been "at the whisky". Patty told her she was "jumpier than a toad". Mary said, "It is surely the fine day," but in truth she was convinced that if she stopped talking for a single moment she would scream. The words, "It was Luke, it was Luke, all the time it was Luke, not old ones," churned around and around in her head. It was as though the earth had shifted, leaving her clinging by a thin vine to the edge of a cliff that had, only seconds before, been a wide pasture.

Evening came. Mary milked the cow but there was less milk than usual because her song was so poor. The sheep backed away from her. The geese seemed to be jeering at her, the rooster laughing. She stayed to weave with Mrs. Colliver and the weaving had to be all undone. When the work was done at last she sped home, pursued by the night wind.

When she reached her own door she picked up the bowl she had kept filled with milk for the house *bodach*. She held it for an instant in her two hands, then in a single, rageful gesture she lifted it over her head and hurled it at the moon. In a lull between gusts of wind she heard it splash into the bay.

"There is no *bodach* here," she said. "There is no kelpie riding these sluggish burns––creeks," she corrected herself scornfully. "How could a kelpie live in a *creek*?" She looked towards the big rock down at the point. "There are no fairies here." Shivering, she hurried into the house.

She stirred up her fire, longing for its high orange flame to be, just once, the soft red of a peat fire. She brought out her spindle whorl and her wool but before long they had dropped unnoticed into her lap. The fire crackled and spat, the wind wailed through the chinks in the logs. She hardly heard it. Her thoughts were too loud, too confused. "What kind of a country is it?" she demanded. "Is there none among them who has the two sights? Is it only the Indians who have the gift of healing?—who speak the charms against ill-wishing here? Och, how could there be fairies in this flat, tree-covered place?"

"Not here. Not here," mocked the wind.

There was a knock at the door. Mary froze. The knock came again, louder. She stood up. The spindle whorl rolled across the floor. The knock came again, louder, more insistent. She put her hand to the back of the chair to steady herself.

"Mary, it's me, Luke—and Henry. Mary, are you there?"

Slowly, step by step, she crossed the room, put back the latch, and pulled open the door. There, in a swirl of dry leaves, stood Luke holding Henry by the hand.

"Luke!" Mary had a powerful urge to throw her arms around him. Hastily she stepped back and tripped on the hem of her skirt.

"Steady." Luke grabbed her arm. She jerked away. "Not so glad to see me, I guess," he said wryly.

Mary uttered the first words that came to her. "It is you have been leaving the pigeons and partridges on my table."

"Now, Mary, they wasn't for courting." Luke looked uncomfortable. "I just figured I could be neighbourly without you getting all riled, seeing as how you was so good to us. Henry and me sort of wanted to say thank you."

Mary had forgotten Henry. Huddled under Luke's arm, he looked cold and pinched.

"Come away in, laddie." She took Henry's hand and pulled him into the house. "Here...why Henry, *mo gràdach*!" Even in the dim light she could see that his face was as grey as stone and one eye was swollen and black. "Luke? How...?"

"Him and Sim had a fight."

"But Sim is sixteen years old, Luke, and Henry is only...."

"Seven," Luke finished for her. "That's what we come for. Mary, could Henry come here with you for a time? You and him get along pretty good so I thought mebbe you mightn't mind.'' Luke's shoulders slumped and his face looked very tired. Mary hated seeing him look like that.

"Put the kettle over,'' she ordered him. "Henry, you sit by the fire.'' She led him to her rocking-chair, sat him down, took the shawl from her shoulders, and wrapped it around him. When the water in the kettle had begun to boil she got up and made him a tansy poultice for his eye and a brew of the same herb to soothe him. By the time she had it ready, he was asleep.

All the while she did this, she was wishing Luke away. She did not want to talk to him. She did not even want to look at him. She knew it wasn't fair, knew it wasn't his fault she had thought the old ones had brought all those gifts, but she was angry at him all the same. Furthermore, she couldn't help remembering how she had almost thrown her arms around him just a few minutes earlier, and she was mortified.

But Luke had settled himself at the table. He was watching her. When she had finished putting the poultice on Henry's eye, he said, "I'd have that tea Henry's gone to sleep over, if you don't mind.''

After she had given it to him she sat down across the table. He turned the cup round and round in his hands. He peered into it. His hair was rumpled and standing in tufts all over his head, and he would have been comical but for the deep furrow in his brow, and the despondent downturn of his usually upturned mouth.

"You might as well know,'' he said. "Ma's not so good. Pa gets himself into a right proper lather when she's like this, and when he seen Henry bawling in the corner on account of Sim hit him, he give him another clout and told him to take his snivelling face out of the way and not to bother coming back.''

"He cannot mean that!"

"Naw. Pa's not so bad. He just gets so he can't stand how things are, then he gets himself full of whisky and starts laying for somebody—no matter who. If it wasn't for Sim being such a...anyways, I figure it would be easier for Pa *and* for Henry if he was to come here for a spell."

"Luke, you are good!" The words came, unbidden. Mary rose hastily from the table, picked up the long stick by the fireplace, and began to stir the fire.

"I guess I was too shy to tell you about *that*." He grinned.

"Luke." Mary bit her lip. "It was not that I thought you had come courting. It was.... Och, why do you *have* to be so good?" she cried angrily. She threw the stick into the flames.

Luke set his unfinished tea on the table with a bang. "I'll bring Henry's duds around," he said, and left the house.

Not two minutes later the door burst open again and Luke's scruffy brown head appeared around it. "Would you rather I was mean?" he bellowed, and slammed the door.

"I do not know! I do not know!" Mary cried. Henry stirred.

She flew across the room. He was fast asleep, his swollen eye dark against the pallor of his face, his face dirty and streaked with tears. "There now," she crooned, "there now." She took off his boots, not much more than uppers connected by a few threads to soles so full of holes there wasn't enough shoe leather between them to make one good boot.

"And how you do need a bath," thought Mary as she struggled to carry him to her bed.

She sat up until very late mending Henry's boots with left-over bits of the old blanket she had got from Julia to stuff the chinks in her wall. She didn't make a very good job of it—she had only a small, dull knife and she was not adept at either cutting or fitting. Furthermore, she could not get her needle through even the thin bit of leather that was left on the boot. Cursing the pedlar who had sold her both knife and needle in exchange for a week's wages, she satisfied herself by cutting the cloth and stuffing it into the boots so that at least Henry would not have to walk in the cold in his bare feet. And all the while she worked, Luke's tired, unhappy face got between her and the boots. "I was so unkind," she thought, and did not feel good about it.

Before the sun was up next morning Mary had Henry out in the creek. Over his cries and howls she scrubbed him up and down with the last bit of Julia's old blanket and sluiced as many lice out of his hair as she could manage. Back inside she told him, as she spooned porridge into her wooden dish for him, "We will wash your clothes after school."

Henry said nothing but his face was not only clean— despite the yellow-and-purple swollen eye it was bright as the morning. His hair was soft and, to Mary's surprise, a bit curly. His feet in their blanket-warm boots swung back and forth against the rungs of the chair and he left nothing in the dish.

It was soon apparent that Henry with two good legs and a full belly, and without the threat of Simeon's blows and his father's quick temper, was a different Henry from the waif Mary had met on the dark road, or the worried little boy she had cared for after his fall. Bolstered by the companionship of Moses Openshaw, Benny Bother, and Matthew Colliver, he would giggle and make rude noises. At supper he became so bold he told her he would rather eat "rotted fish than corn mush". When Mary told him it was porridge, he said it was the same as his mother's samp and he wasn't going to eat it for supper. "Then fish for your supper," Mary retorted. He would run off when it was time to prepare for school or clean up afterwards, and hide from Mary at bedtime. It was the running and hiding that bothered Mary. She was afraid for him. It wasn't that she had had an actual premonition but she felt uneasy. She did not want to let him out of her sight.

When Luke bought Henry's spare pants and shirt, and a knitted jacket and threadbare blanket that Mary suspected really belonged to Luke himself, she tried to tell him that there was danger and that Henry might be better off home after all.

"Don't you want him here, Mary?"

"I do!" Mary did not think Luke would believe there was a devil's voice that called to her in the night but she did not want to send Henry home either. She loved his bright chatter, their shared meals, loved telling him stories—stories of fairies and kelpies and urisks and the magic of the unseen world, stories about her own childhood and the people she had known back in her glen. She liked teaching Henry to read and write, delighting in the way his face lit when he had managed to write a letter or read a word.

"I do want him here," she told Luke and she longed to add, "and I will be glad if you will come to see him." She wanted to tell him she was sorry she had been unkind, but she was proud.

Luke did come frequently to take Henry fishing or hunting or just out into the woods with him. Sometimes they came back with a rabbit or a grouse or partridge, "for Henry's board," he would tell Mary stiffly. The only other conversation he offered in ten days was to say, after he had taken Henry fishing one afternoon, "Henry ain't a baby, you can give him a bit of slack."

But Mary was afraid of a bit of slack. The headache that always presaged danger had begun. Every afternoon that Luke did not come she took Henry to the Collivers' with her, and she made him promise that he would not ever go near the big grey rock down on the point.

She wished Owena would come so that she could talk to her about the spirits. But the Indians had gone off in their canoes to the mainland where the big game was.

One crisp afternoon in early November, when the leaves were gone from the hardwood trees, when all the flowers but the Michaelmas daisies had blackened under the frost and only the late apples were still on the boughs, Henry pleaded with Mary to let him go with Moses Openshaw to his grandfather's cider mill five miles north of Collivers' Corners. Mary saw both the rebellion and the longing in his eyes, thought how safe he would surely be at Moses' grandfather's, and said he might go.

She was washing Mrs. Colliver's china teapot when the dizziness came. The teapot crashed to the floor. Mary slumped against the table. She recovered at once. Still clutching the dish rag, she ran from the house. Her heart thumping, a prayer repeating itself in her head, she raced down the road. She reached her meadow and stumbled across it to the point. Henry was floating face down in the water.

In one frantic movement Mary fell to her knees, scooped him out of the water, turned him over her knees, and whacked him again and again on his back with all the strength she had.

For a few moments Henry made no response. Then he began to sputter and gasp and spew water. His arms flailed and he arched his back. Furiously Mary went on pounding until he began to cry. Then she leapt to her feet, dragging him with her. She set him on his feet and shook him. Her hair had come loose from its braid and was blowing around her face in long, black, wet strings, tears were running down her cheeks, and her clothes were almost as wet as Henry's.

"How could you?" she cried. "I told you, Henry, I told you. You promised me. Yon water is black. It is evil. Do you never, never go near it again should you live to be five hundred years and more. Do you understand?" By now she was shouting in Gaelic, *am feasd*! never! never! and a lot more Henry could not possibly understand. His teeth chattered, his head was bobbing dangerously on his neck, and his eyes were huge with terror. Water streamed from his clothes.

For a second Mary relaxed her grip. Henry pulled loose. Sobbing, he ran up past the house, across the road, and into the deep woods.

"Come back," shouted Mary. "You come back!" But Henry did not. Mary raced after him. At the edge of the forest she stopped short. She took a deep breath and tried to force herself into the trees, but no matter how she tried, she could not make her feet take another step.

"Henry," she screamed, "come away out of there."

There was no reply.

"Henry!" She waited. Her ragged breath began to slow. "Henry!" She pushed her wet hair from her face, wiped her tears with her sleeve. Her voice softened. "Henry, *please*."

Nothing.

"Henry, do you not see how feared I was? I did not mean to hurt you but you were set to drown. Och, Henry, I do care so much for you. Please, *mo gràdach*, come away out of the trees."

Nothing.

Numbly Mary sat down on the road. She drew her knees up and rested her head on them. In a few moments she began again. She called, cajoled, and pleaded for almost an hour. Then Luke came swinging along the road, a partridge over his shoulder.

"Luke!" Stiffly Mary got to her feet. "Henry..." Mary began.

"What's happened?" Luke grabbed her by the shoulders and she thought, for a second, that he was going to shake her as she had shaken Henry.

"He is not hurt," she said quickly, "but Luke, he has gone into the forest and he will not come out."

Luke stared at her, open-mouthed. "Are you so afraid of the woods you won't go fetch him?"

"I am." Mary was too upset, too tired, to let his words hurt her pride.

Luke plunged into the woods and was soon back, grim-faced, dragging Henry. Henry's face was red and swollen from crying, his lips were blue, and his teeth were chattering. His clothes were still wet. Timidly Mary put her hand towards him but Luke did not stop. He trotted Henry across the road and into Mary's cabin. Mary followed, her footsteps slow, her body drained of all thought and feeling.

Inside Luke sat down on the first school bench. He stood Henry before him, holding him with an iron grip.

"Luke," Mary began hesitantly. He paid no attention.

"What set you hiding from Mary?" he demanded.

"She—she shaked me."

"How come?"

"I got drowned."

"What?"

"I went into the water where she said I wasn't to," Henry whispered.

"You fell in?"

Henry nodded. Luke looked at Mary's tired face, her wet, bedraggled state. "Did Mary have to fetch you out?"

Henry nodded again. By this time Luke's face was as white as Henry's. Deliberately he stripped off

151

Henry's wet clothes, turned him over his knee, and spanked him hard, three times. Then he stood him up. Henry's chin quivered, but he made no sound. He did not look at either Luke or Mary.

"He got any clean duds?" Luke demanded.

Mary brought them, although by now she had begun to resent the fact that Luke had had to rescue Henry, that Luke had had to discipline him.

"Luke, I can take care of him."

"Henry, look at me."

Henry looked up.

"Henry, I ain't whupped you on account of you fell in the bay. I whupped you on account of you ran off and hid where you knew Mary wasn't going to come. Do you see that?"

Henry nodded.

"You got something to say?"

Henry shook his head.

"Well...." Luke pushed a hand through his thick hair. "If you ain't hot enough from the hiding, you best go set by the fire." He left the house.

He was back within two minutes. "Some varmint got the bird I brung for your suppers," he said disgustedly.

Still shaking from cold and fear, Mary had put the kettle over the fire. When she saw Luke about to leave again she said, "There will be salmon and tatties and squash and berry tart enough for three." Then she climbed the ladder to the loft to change her own clothes, wishing she hadn't run from the Collivers' without her plaid.

They ate their dinner with few words spoken. Afterwards Mary went outside to bring water from the creek. Luke followed her.

"You could let me carry it," he said quietly. Mary gave him the kettle and stood shivering while he dipped water into it from the bark bucket.

"Be ice over the creek by morning," he said. "Ain't you got a wrap?"

"I left it at the Collivers'." Suddenly Mary felt warmer. Luke had forgiven her for speaking so unkindly to him the night he'd brought Henry to her. "Luke, he was floating—" The catch in her throat stopped her words.

"I figured."

They went back into the house. Henry had gone up to the loft where he slept. On the table was the bit of bark Mary had given him on which to practise his writing. He had written on it, "NO STORIE". Mary dropped into the chair and put her head down on the piece of bark. Luke stood with his hands in his pants pockets, whistling under his breath.

After a time Mary raised her head. She stood up. Resolutely she faced him. "There is something here," she said. "There is an evil spirit, Luke. It lives in that bit of water and it calls to me. It calls in Duncan's voice but it is not Duncan and I am afraid. I was afraid for Henry. I tried to watch him, but it reached out for him. I know you will think I am daft but I am not." Braving the incredulous expression on his face, she continued. She told him again about having the gift of the two sights. She told him about growing up in the hills with Duncan, about Duncan's leaving home, and about hearing him call after four years. She told him about Mrs. Grant's prophecy. She told him that she was learning to spin and weave properly so that she could earn her way home. She told him again about seeing Dan Pritch-ett's barn on fire and locking herself in the privy so that she wouldn't have to warn anyone, and about seeing him, Luke, carrying Henry, and how she had seen his mother in the snow. She told him that she needed to be in Duncan's house, "to feel his presence once more, to know he is at peace. But there is only the black thing that calls and calls me in Duncan's voice." Her voice was low and throbbing. "And it would have taken Henry if I had not known—and I broke Julia Colliver's grandmother's teapot so I may not have work now." She told him, at last, that she had thought the gifts he had brought had been gifts from the fairies, the old ones. "And it was good of you, Luke, and I was without thanks or kindness and I am sorry for it." She stopped. She drew a deep breath and waited as though for a verdict.

"You kind of took care of Duncan, didn't you?" was Luke's only reply.

"I did not. It was Duncan who was the strong one. He did not like that I had the two sights but he did not look askint at me as some do."

"I wish I could make you feel better about him being gone and I wish I hadn't of talked to you about marrying when you was still so sore grieved," said Luke. "I don't know about all of them other things you was saying. I see you really believe they're so and I guess I've got no cause to say they ain't. I know others—the O'Haras and their old gran down to Soames and Mrs. Hennessey at the Corners—talk like that but it always sounds like yarning to me. I guess I can't say you don't see the things you say you do,'' he conceded with obvious reluctance. ''I guess I just don't know. I mean, folks hereabouts won't let a load of hay go by without wishing on it and they look at a new moon with a mite of caution—careful about black cats crossing in front of them and the like, too, on account of nobody wants to cross Old Mr. Scratch, just on the chance of spending all hereafter jumping hot coals for him. There's plenty of folk who talk about ghosts and there's sure plenty with an appetite for grisly stories. But the way you talk about them things, you make ghosts and them strange critters and such sound like they're neighbours. It's downright scary to hear you sometimes, Mary. But when it comes to something in the bay that's out to get Henry—come on. You can easy let your sad feelings about this place make all sorts of things plague you. You'd be a sight better off if you was to put some of them ideas away. And Mary,'' he added, in such a low voice she had to strain to hear him, ''you'd be a sight better off if you was to live somewhere else.''

Mary looked up. In Luke's eyes was an unmistakable look of love. He cleared his throat. ''Henry won't go near that patch of water again, you can bet your life.'' He moved towards the door. ''And Mary, if it'll make you feel better I'll keep my eye on Ma. Good night.''

Mary stood where she was for a long time after Luke had gone. No one had ever looked at her like that. She had known that the boys who had come courting at home had cared about her. And there had always been Duncan, so much a part of her she had never thought about how he felt about her. But Luke was different—disturbing.

When Henry got up the next morning he did not favour Mary with looks of love. He would answer "yes" or "no" to everything she asked and that was all.

"He is like Luke," Mary thought exasperatedly. "When he is crossed he does not speak." When Duncan was angry, he would say he would not speak but his words would come stinging like a hive of wasps. The thought flicked through her mind that she liked Henry's—and Luke's—way better.

She sat down with Henry the morning after the accident and tried to get him to tell her how it had happened but he would only say, "I don't know." She told him she was sorry she had shaken him so, to which he said nothing.

But on the evening of the third day he came to her after supper. He stood in front of her chair.

"If a body drownds dead, can they still walk?" he asked.

"It cannot." Mary put down her spinning. "It must lie in a wooden box cold and still as baby did when he died, and then be buried in the ground."

Henry burst into tears. Mary took him on her lap and they comforted each other for the thing that had almost happened but had not.

CHAPTER XII
A Swift Magic

In the middle of the night Mary was wakened by a strange sound. She sat up, listening. From somewhere there came a deep, slow boom—boom—boom. She got out of bed, threw her plaid around her shoulders, went outside, and gasped from the cold.

The moon was full. The sky was clear. There was no wind. The ground was covered with a crackling silver-white frost. Each blade of grass, each stand of yarrow, tansy and milkweed, each twig and branch of every bush and every tree glistened in the bright, white light. The bay had frozen smooth and hard, as though a hand had pulled a sheet of glass over it.

There were no animal sounds, no bird sounds. Even the wolves in the forest had stopped howling. In all the world there was only that eerie boom—

boom—boom and it came from somewhere deep in the bay. It seemed that, in the silence that had come over the woods and the water, the earth's heartbeat could at last be heard.

Mary felt she had surprised a moment in the earth's turning that no person was meant to witness. Yet, at the same time, she felt herself to be such a part of the turning that she could feel no separation between herself, the earth, the sky, the water, and that booming heartbeat that gave life to them all. A tremor ran through her, she became aware of her separate self once more, and of the piercing cold. Shivering but full of joy, she stayed for another few minutes, dancing up and down to warm herself.

Back inside, she built up the fire and sat for a while, her body warmed, her spirit full of wonder. While she did not clearly form the thoughts in her head, she felt that the heartbeat of the fairy hill in her own Highland glen and the one deep in Hawthorn Bay were the same. "Surely nothing bad can happen to me now?" she whispered and went to bed smiling.

Henry woke her in the morning. "We got winter!" he crowed. "Get up! Get up! We got winter. Mary, wake up!" He pulled her nose.

Mary laughed out loud. She gave him a shove and got out of bed. "We did get winter." She shivered as her feet touched the cold, rough boards. "I saw it come in the night, Henry. It came in a swift magic." She gave him his jacket and her wool stockings, stuffed her own bare feet into her shoes, wrapped herself in her plaid, and out they went to explore the winter.

The bay was silent in the bright sunlight but the sparrows and juncos were twittering in the shimmering bushes and among the branches of the willow and birch trees along the shore. Frost still covered everything and the cold had made the air so clear the houses and barns across the bay could be seen through the bare limbs of the hardwood trees as though they were only a few feet away. Henry ran to slide on the ice. Across the bay the Morrissay and Bother and Heaton children were shouting happily and doing the same. There would be no school this day. Mary stood on the big grey rock and looked down through the ice at the leaves and twigs caught there, and at her own reflection, as clear as though seen in a fine silver-backed mirror.

She saw, to her surprise, that she looked like the same girl who had once, many ages ago, looked at herself in the waters of Loch Ness—the same black hair and eyes, same pale complexion, same little nose and wide mouth—but this girl's hair was in a braid hanging over one shoulder, the way the Canadian girls wore theirs, and somehow, though it had really only been six months, this girl looked older. The corner of her mouth twitched and she smiled. "I think," she murmured, "nothing bad can happen to me now." She ran out onto the ice after Henry.

They chased and slid and laughed and suddenly there was Luke rounding the corner of the cabin with a bundle in his arms. With a whoop he dropped the bundle and raced down to the bay. Zeke Pritchett's puppy came barking out onto the ice in front of Mary. Down they went together. Mary's shawl got tangled around the dog until he became a writhing mass of wool and tail on the ice, yipping and howling through the thick cloth. Finally Mary managed to unroll the wriggling dog from his prison. He was so happy to see the world again that he jumped at her face, licked her nose, her eyes, her mouth, and knocked her flat on her back.

"Och," Mary laughed self-consciously. She stood up, brushing herself off, and looked at Luke. He smiled happily at her.

"We have not had our breakfasts yet," she said. "Henry will be getting cold. Come away in now, Henry."

"One more slide," pleaded Henry.

Half an hour later, over their bread and porridge and a bit of fish left from supper, Mary told Luke about the strange booming in the night.

"It's always like that when the freeze-up comes sudden. I don't know why but it is." Luke's face echoed the wonder Mary had felt. "It ain't easy, this here country, but it's grand," he went on. "When Pa and Ma come here there wasn't nothing but wilderness on the whole island, or anywhere else this side of Lake Ontario—or the other, I guess—just trees." He grinned at Mary. "And beaver meadows like this one, or swamps that got burned out by lightning. Grandpa and Grandma Anderson and Grandpa and Grandma Grissom all made their places more'n thirty miles from here—down near South Bay. Nice farms they got started. Pa was the youngest boy and there wasn't room for him, so after him and Ma got married and got the grants the government gives all them as was children of the Loyalists, they come along up here. Pa's all but killing himself making that farm and Ma....'' He stopped. He stuck his thumbs into his suspenders. ''Well, you know how it is with Ma. Nope, it ain't easy country, that's sure, but it's beautiful the way winter comes all shining and spring comes a-rushing in, and summer in the woods is something grand. You might get to like it if you was to give it a try.''

Mary could imagine Luke in the summer woods, his russet hair, his tanned face, and his easy stride, as much a part of his surroundings as the squirrels or the deer.

''I might.''

''Henry,'' said Luke, ''Pa's mending harness and cleaning the stalls this morning. I have a mind to go grouse hunting. D'you want to come?''

''Yep, I do.'' Henry's face lit up and he scrambled from his bench.

After they had gone Mary sat for a while, hearing the silence they had left behind. The day was still beautiful but suddenly it had lost its excitement.

The cold did not abate and winter came up the bay in gales and snow. Mary found that her old plaid was not much protection against the bitter cold of Upper Canada and that her feet were red and stiff. When Owena came next, Mary traded some of her rough weaving and a few oat bannocks for warm deerskin moccasins for Henry and herself. She knew the trade was probably unfair but her feet were cold and she was afraid Henry would get sick and she promised Owena she would make it right as soon as she could.

Owena walked around the snow-covered meadow examining the shoreline carefully. She stopped to peer into the ice by the big rock. She came back to where Mary stood just outside the door. "It sleeps like the bear," she said, "that's good."

The neighbourhood, however, was wide awake. Snow covered the stony, rutted, rough roads, smoothing them so that sledges, cutters, and horse- or ox-drawn sleighs could move easily. Ice covered all the waterways so that feet and sleighs and even wagons could cross them, although there were weak spots and drivers needed to be very careful. The settlers had learned from the Indians to make and use snowshoes for travelling readily over the snow.

Winter evenings were visiting times. Luke came frequently to Mary's house, "to help Henry with his lessons," he insisted, but one time when Mary asked him to read over what Henry was trying aloud, Luke confessed, flushing with embarrassment, "I can't read. I was kind of hoping I could learn it alongside Henry."

Mary was astonished. It was not in Upper Canada as it was in the Highlands, Luke told her—schools were not commonplace: Dan Pritchett was an exceptional man and the children in his neighbourhood were very lucky. She was not sure about having Luke for a pupil, though at the same time she was rather pleased that she knew something he wanted to learn. "You ain't to thump me if I get it wrong," Luke told her and his face was so solemn when he said it, Mary was sure he was serious. "I would need to ask you to get to your knees to manage it." She saw the grin on his face, and made a face back at him. "I will teach you," she said.

Many evenings Patty Openshaw came up the road with a pile of family mending to do by Mary's fire, and once in a while Simeon came, interrupting the lessons with his loud, derisive laughter, demanding supper, demanding attention. Then Patty would sit herself between Simeon and Luke and jolly them along until Simeon either left or settled down to listen to the story-telling or take part in the conversation. Mercifully he did not come often, finding such quiet company not much to his liking, and so the four of them—Patty, Mary, Luke and Henry—developed a warm, almost family-like kind of companionship.

Even those evenings when the little house held only Mary and Henry were pleasant. She would spin while he read close to the fire that warmed such a small radius of space, leaving the edges of the room almost as cold as outdoors. On snowy, windy nights, the snow blew in through the cracks, but the wind that whistled and sang and sometimes moaned did not call Mary away.

Christmas came. There were festive gatherings in all the households, culminating in a feast on Christmas Day at Sam and Julia Colliver's. Early Christmas morning Mary took Henry to the Pritchetts' where Dan was having prayers and a Bible reading. All the Hawthorn Bay families were there and Mary offered a private prayer of thanks for the kindness of neighbours. Afterwards she and Henry went early to the Collivers' to help — although Henry's help amounted to bringing in large piles of wood with Matthew for the fireplaces, then racing off outside to slide and run in the snow.

Mrs. Colliver had been very angry about her smashed teapot. But when Mary explained about Henry's accident she had said only, ''Hmph,'' and looked at Mary from under a frown. She had said no more and she had not dismissed Mary from her job. On Christmas morning she was organizing and ordering Mary, Patty, and her own children about with the skill and authority of a regimental sergeant-major. As they passed one another bearing platters, silverware, and dishes of condiments, Patty and Mary smiled happily at one another, rolling their eyes towards the ceiling as each new order was barked.

The party was wonderful. Bothers and Heatons and Morrissays came from the south shore of Hawthorn Bay; Openshaws, Pritchetts and Yardleys from the north shore; Whitcombs, Schneiders, and Andersons from Pigeon Creek Road; Mrs. Hazen and her daughters; Obadiah Clark, who lived alone; and Hennessys, Bartons, and Armstrongs from the village. There were others whose names Mary could not remember—children of all ages, mothers, fathers, aunts, uncles, grandparents, and a few great-grandparents—and they all sat down to eat at the long trestle tables stretched from the back wall of the kitchen to the front wall of the front room, and angled out across the hall and into the front bedroom.

Julia was wearing her best plum-coloured silk gown, with a fine lawn kerchief at her neck and a pinafore to protect the gown. It had become a bit small over the years, and strained mightily at the seams. This only accentuated the amplitude of her figure, and with the addition of a large rose-satin bow on her head, its streamers floating down her back, she was like a goddess of plenty presiding over the celebration. Sam, as splendid in his worn rust-velvet waistcoat and bottle-green coat, was less imposing but every bit as hospitable.

The guests were dressed in a motley assortment of pre-1775 finery and homespun, valiantly embellished with a ribbon, a treasured lace fichu here, a sprig of evergreen or a nosegay of dried flowers there.

The house was decorated with garlands of cedar and pine, lighted by more than fifty candles, the tables covered with an assortment of linen cloths belonging to several families. There were wild turkeys and dooryard geese, roasted; there were boiled and roasted potatoes. There were pumpkins and squash, baked and glazed with maple sugar; there was fine white bread; and there were the fruit preserves which Patty and Mary had laboured over, baked into cakes, puddings, and pies; and with them whisky, cider, and a bit of carefully saved real tea and coffee to drink. Mary had never dreamed of such food.

"In this country," she thought as she looked along the enormous table, "there is food in plenty for all, there is clean water to drink, and there is so much space no one need ever think of having to leave just to keep body and soul together.'' The wish that her whole family could be seated at that table brought a lump to her throat. She swallowed it back and, resolutely, did not think about Duncan. She looked at Henry seated across from her beside his mother, making faces at Moses Openshaw and Matthew Colliver sitting at the foot of the table. She smiled. ''It is no bad place,'' she thought, and glanced involuntarily towards Luke sitting on the other side of his mother, talking to Zeke Colliver. Luke, no doubt feeling her eyes on him, turned his head and caught her glance. Despite herself, she was glad of the scarlet ribbon Mrs. Colliver had given her to tie around her black hair.

Afterwards there were games, riddles, stories, and songs. In his uneven tenor voice Luke led the singing of a round, Dan Pritchett sang ''Barbara Allen'' in his beautiful baritone voice, and Mary, loosed from her reticence by the friendliness of her neighbours and the excitement of the occasion, sang ''The Rowan Tree'' and ''Lovely Molly''. Abe Morrissay's father, Jim, picked out the melody on his fiddle. After that the tables were cleared and carried away and everyone danced to Jim's fiddling. Mary danced every dance and didn't mind when the young men teased her about being small, because she was so nimble they had a hard time keeping up with her.

The party settled at last. Those bent on carousing the night away went off up the road to one house or another for their party. The children went to sleep—in nests in corners, or on the beds behind the kitchen, or upstairs. The women began to wash the dishes. The men sat over their whisky and their coffee. When they began to talk of spring planting and next year's harvest, Mary, coming from the scullery with a handful of silverware, saw an image of the gardens blighted and black from frost. "There will be no summer next year," she said.

There was a moment of silence, surprised laughter, then the talk resumed. In the kitchen Julia scolded her. "Don't you make such a fool of yourself, my girl. Do you want the entire neighbourhood to think you're not right in the head?" Mary said nothing.

Luke found her alone in the scullery not long afterwards.

"You're kind of quiet." He did not wait for a response. Self-consciously he brought something out of his pocket. "You look nice in that red ribbon," he said. "Here, I got something for you." He held out a tiny, carved wooden loon. It was not finely done but there was life in the set of it and in its round black dots of eyes.

Mary looked at it in Luke's outstretched hand and did not take it from him at once.

"Don't you like it?" His voice wasn't much more than a whisper.

"I do," she breathed. "Luke, it looks like the bird himself. But..." she blurted, "I am ashamed."

"Ashamed?"

"I have no gifts. I did not know it was meant. We do not do so at Christmas at home. Mrs. Morrissay across the bay has given me a packet of tea. Mrs. Colliver gave me this ribbon and made for me a warm bonnet and Patty brought me a dish filled to the brim with maple sugar and Sarah Pritchett gave me a bit of slate and a fine embroidered handkerchief.'' She looked helplessly at Luke.

"It don't signify, Mary.''

"It do, Luke.'' She had to laugh.

"Are you going to say you won't take it?''

"I am not.'' She held out her hand, and Luke placed the little carving in it. She stroked the tiny wings, and closed her fingers around it.

When it was time to go home the Pritchetts found room to tuck Mary and Henry into their sleigh. "It was a fine gift to us all, your singing,'' Sarah whispered to Mary as they rode along behind the jingling sleigh bells and the sleepy voices of Dan and Martha talking.

"I will never forget this day, if there come to be three thousand and more in my life,'' declared Mary passionately. Impulsively she put her arms around Sarah and kissed her cheek.

"Well,'' said Sarah, and nothing more, but Mary knew she was pleased.

CHAPTER XIII
"So Cold"

The year ended with no special mark. Mary sat down and wrote a letter home, thinking wistfully all day of the Hogmanay celebrations in the glen. Carefully she put it aside with the others she was saving to send when the ice broke and ships came up the lake again.

But one evening, not long after, Mary was having a lesson with Luke and Henry when she had a second, clear vision of Lydia Anderson struggling through blinding snow.

"Luke." Mary put the book down. "Maybe tomorrow would do for Henry to see his mother."

"Why so sudden?"

"It is a fair bit of time since he has been home, I am thinking."

"I figured on going off hunting tomorrow. I

thought mebbe I'd take him along with me.''

"I have seen your mother in the snow again, Luke," Mary said.

"Aw, Mary. I don't want you get all riled, honest to God I don't, but I wish you wouldn't go around saying things like that. People will think you got bats in your belfry...."

Mary jumped up, her eyes bright with anger. "Do you think I like the pictures? Do you think I am happy to see what will be when others do not? Do folk care for me the more? They do not. You think I am daft, I can see you do, but I see what I see, I have promised myself and all the powers that be that I will not flinch from telling it, and I have seen your mother in dire need, and do you not take Henry to see her this very day I will take him myself."

"Now, Mary—"

"I will take him myself, Luke."

"Henry," he said, "I guess mebbe we'll go see Ma. We might as well go tonight. If we don't your Miss Mary's going to set out and cause no end of mischief."

Henry unglued himself from his chair.

"I ain't going."

"Git," said Luke.

While Mary watched unhappily, Luke bundled Henry up and they left. Henry returned the next day to tell Mary that Sim had teased him because he was cleaned up. "He called me a pretty little girl. I hate Sim!" He said nothing about his mother.

Three weeks later, in a wild blizzard, Lydia Anderson wandered out into the woods and froze to death. Mary took Henry to the brief ceremony, watching sadly as the pine box was carried into the woods to be put into the hut until spring, when the ground would be thawed for the burial.

His arm across Henry's shoulder, John Anderson thanked Mary for having Henry to stay with her. "Things was pretty bad around here for the little feller," he admitted. "I guess we don't always pull together so well." He asked if she would mind keeping him with her a little while longer. "He seems to be getting along all right and his ma sure admired to have him get the schooling."

"He can stay." Mary was unable to tell John how much it meant to her to have Henry with her.

"She's not coming back no more never, is she?" Henry asked afterwards, when they were back in the Hawthorn Bay house.

"No," said Luke. He had walked them home and they were having tea by the fire—Henry on his low stool, Mary in her rocking-chair, Luke on the bench he had drawn up to the hearth. "She wasn't happy in this world, Henry, maybe God will look after her better in the next."

"Will she be with them folks that's got all them silver bells?"

"What's them?"

"You know. Them folks you can't see that Mary tells about with their green clothes and silver bells and magic horses."

Luke glanced at Mary. He frowned. "I don't know. I ain't never been dead."

"Will she haunt me?"

"No, she won't."

Luke stayed until after Henry had gone to bed. "Mary—" He was clearly upset. "Mary, I know how

171

you care about all them stories about fairies and magic and ghosts, but I'm feared for Henry. Especially right now when Ma's only just died. He scares awful easy, Henry does."

Mary drew a sharp breath. There it was again, stories. Luke meant nonsense as Julia Colliver had meant nonsense, as Sarah Pritchett had meant nonsense. She thrust her chin forward defensively but she said nothing.

"I don't want to make you feel bad, honest I don't." Luke's face was puckered into a worried frown and his brown eyes were troubled. "But I can't just go along with some of what you say. I'd like to."

"I do not mind." Mary's back was stiff, her voice controlled.

"I don't know! Dang blast it! I know you figured you was seeing into the future when you said Ma was going to die but I can't rightly say that's strange. We could all see it was bound to happen."

"Luke, it was not only your mother, it was Henry drowning in the bay, it was him falling from the tree, it was the Pritchetts' barn burning, it was Polly in the barn. Do not all those things tell you something?"

"Well…." Luke hesitated. "Well, mebbe they was happen-chance and mebbe…."

"And maybe I was spinning a tale for you." Mary's voice was tart. She glowered at him.

He glowered back. "I guess mebbe I'd better be getting along home."

"I guess mebbe you'd better," she mimicked.

After he had left, Mary felt a pang of remorse that she had lost her temper. "Him with his mother just dead," she thought. She almost ran after him to say she was sorry; but it was very dark that night, and cold, and she knew how fast his long, strong legs would take him—and through the woods, too.

Henry came in the night to Mary's bed. "I don't want her ghostus to haunt me," he cried. "She's gonna come after me."

"Henry," Mary asked gently, "did your mother ever come after you in your life?"

"No."

"Why did she not?"

"She just didn't."

"It maybe was because she was a sweet and gentle person who did not go chasing after folk."

"Mebbe," sniffed Henry.

"Then, Henry, why do you think she will come after you now she has died?"

"Not her—her ghostus."

"Why would the ghost of a gentle person like your mother be so hateful?"

"Ghostuses ain't nice."

"Some are. If the ghost of your mother walks abroad, it might be she wants to see that her boys are cared for."

Reluctantly Henry agreed that it might be, but for weeks he woke in the middle of the night and came scuttling down the ladder to make a dive for the safety of Mary's bed.

Winter retreated slowly. March brought the worst storms of the season, blizzards with winds that threw roof-high drifts against the sides of the little houses and across the roads and paths, and made miniature drifts inside the houses in all the corners. For almost two weeks Mary and Henry could get no farther than the hole they had cut in the ice on the creek for their water. They were growing tired of eating soft, sprouting potatoes and cornmeal mush. They were frantic from being cooped up. Finally they amused each other by digging tunnels through the drifts with their hands.

Then one day there was the welcome sound of water dripping from the roof and the trees. There was another freeze and a thaw, the crows and jays came out of the swamp to call and screech, the sap began to run in the trees, and it was sugaring-time. Everyone in the community was off into the woods where the sugar huts had been built. Every sugar-maple tree in the forest had been tapped. Mary longed to see how the sap was boiled, to join in the fun of pouring the hot syrup onto the snow to eat. She could hear the laughter cascading like birdsong out of the woods. But she could not go into the forest. Every time she tried, terror gripped her heart, her breath choked in her throat, and her feet froze.

Luke shook his head disbelievingly. Julia Colliver was cross. Henry came running one day with sugar-taffy sticky in his bare hands to where Mary sat, ashamed and unhappy, on the big grey rock, watching the water move under the ice.

"Henry," she said, "you are a kind boy."

"Luke sent some, too." He took a lump covered with lint and dirt from his pocket.

"I will save Luke's," Mary told him, "and eat yours."

The ice broke up in April. The children from across the bay came again in row-boats, wrapped in

174

shawls, their fur hats covering their heads against the chill winds that still blew constantly down the bay. The wild geese and ducks came back to their summer nesting-grounds in the swamps and marshes. The great blue herons were right behind them. Their harsh gronk-gronk-gronk sounded to Mary, as it mingled with the higher tones of the ducks and geese, like fiddlers tuning up for the dance—discordant, exciting, inviting summer to come.

There were buds on all the trees, as soft and pale green as they had always been at home. Mary sang as she washed her clothes in the creek and helped the Collivers' ewes give birth to their lambs—but she thought often of the time only a year past when she had been doing the same in the pasture at home.

The last ice to break up was the ice around the point by the big grey rock. The dark water emerged from its ice prison to slap menacingly against the rock.

Owena returned that day. She said nothing about the black water. She said only, "We are not far," and Mary took comfort from her words.

Late that night the beseeching voice called again, "Come, Mairi, come!"

She was determined not to hear it. She concentrated on her spinning, which had progressed from bits of thin-thick knobs and strings not much longer than her forearm to skeins of yarn as even and fine as silk—and she had woven a length of cloth on Julia Colliver's loom that was smooth enough to offer for sale. But it was hard not to rise from her chair and follow wherever that voice so like Duncan's might lead.

Henry heard only the wind and, blissfully unaware of Mary's anguish, he chattered in the evenings about the tadpoles he had found in the swamp, the pussywillows that blossomed along the shore, and old Jake Armstrong who had almost disappeared in the mud "right out in front of Miz Hazen's store".

The mud was terrible. Neither sledges nor carts could navigate the road and most people travelled through the woods. Mary kept to the road's edge, hopping from one root to the next, one stone to another, as though she were fording a stream. The children sang happily, "Mud time, mud time, six weeks to bare feet." The only benefit the soft ground brought was that when the Methodist circuit preacher arrived in the neighbourhood the winter's dead could be buried. Lydia Anderson's body was put to rest beside the bodies of her babies. Henry cried for his mother then. After that, he stopped having bad dreams.

People began talking of planting and Mary saw once more the blighted fields and vegetable patches, the frost-blackened trees and frozen fledgeling birds. She told Luke. She told Mrs. Colliver. She told Dan Pritchett. Luke was kinder than the others—he said nothing. Dan laughed and patted her on the head, which made her furious. "Keep such thoughts in your head," Mrs. Colliver told her sharply.

As the days wore into weeks it grew colder. Mary's head began to ache again, and her voice took on a sharp edge. In her state of anxiety she forgot the promise she had made to Sarah Pritchett, and, more and more, the stories she told the children had to do with witches and spells and terrible accidents. One day, after the children had gone home, Sarah spoke to her about it and Mary burst into tears.

"What matter?" she cried. "I might as well spin fancy yarns, I cannot make a breathing soul listen to what I know and all the planting will come to naught. There will be no summer, Sarah, I have seen that."

"There, there," said Sarah nervously, "oh dear, we'll have some tea, don't cry."

Mary laughed. "Sarah Pritchett, however can you manage to teach at all when the sound of me weeping frightens you so? Och, *Dia*, I do not mean to frighten the children."

One evening, after Henry had gone to bed, Simeon burst through the door. "All alone?" He dragged a chair from the table to sit beside her. He was stinking of whisky.

Mary nodded and went on with her spinning. "Ain't you gonna smile?" He grinned at her. "Ain't you even gonna offer a fellow something to drink?"

Mary decided it might be wise to give him something to kill the effect of the whisky. She went to the larder and took out several corncakes, a bit of cheese, and the ground dandelion roots that made a kind of coffee. She put the food on the table, the grounds in the kettle, and swung the kettle over the fire.

"Come along then," she said curtly.

"Naw. You keep them things. I want a drink of whisky. Come on, Mary." He jumped up clumsily, knocking over his chair. He grabbed her around the waist.

For a second she went rigid. Then, carefully and firmly, she moved away. Simeon threw one arm around her shoulders, yanked her head back by her hair with his free hand, and kissed her mouth. Mary shoved. Simeon was large and strong but he was drunk. Mary was small but she was strong too, and sure-footed. She darted to the other side of the table and picked up the knife she had put out for cutting cheese. "I do not think you will be foolish, Simeon Anderson, but if you come after me, it is your ears I will be putting out for the wild beasts to feed on. You will be glad then not to be seen more in this neighbourhood."

"It's true what they say. You're a queer one, all right." He sneered. "I guess you give my brother all the fun."

The door flew open and Patty Openshaw burst into the room with Luke right behind her. She threw off her cloak and ran to stand by the fire, rubbing her hands together, stamping her feet. "I was coming along for a dish of tea when I met up with Luke and now here's Sim. Is that coffee I smell?"

Luke had been looking at Mary, at Sim, at the knife Mary held in her hand. With one step he crossed the floor. "Go home, Sim," he said. He sounded as though he were talking to a disobedient dog. Sim started to say something, looked at Luke, pushed past him to snatch his coat from the bench where he'd thrown it, and grabbed the door latch.

"Come on, Patty." He jerked his head towards the door. "I'll walk you home."

Patty had been watching the scene, her mouth open, her eyes wide. Before she could reply Mary said, "You'll have your coffee, Patty." Her voice was steady.

Patty looked at Luke. Something in the way he was standing, saying nothing, watching Mary, decided her.

"I guess mebbe I'll get along home now, too," she said, the laughter and excitement gone from her voice.

A log fell forward onto the hearth. Mary took the stick and pushed it back. She felt a sudden sharpness in her never-ending headache, then the momentary dizziness. In the flames she saw Patty weeping.

She spun around. "Do not go yet, Patty. Luke shall walk along with you when you have had coffee and a bit to eat."

Patty smiled with an obvious effort. "I guess I won't stop." She picked up her cloak and shrugged herself into it.

"Do not go!" Mary shot across the room and grabbed Patty by the arm.

"I ain't stopping, Mary." Patty put Mary's restraining hand from her.

Simeon grinned triumphantly, bowed deeply to Mary and Luke, took Patty by the hand, and led her through the door. Mary started to follow them, stopped, turned to Luke.

"Go after them," she pleaded.

"Do you want Sim to stay?"

"Luke, I am afraid for Patty!"

"She's safe enough."

179

"But I saw, Luke."

"You saw! You saw! Mary, Patty Openshaw can look out for herself."

"If Patty is safe with your brother, Luke Anderson, then so am I and you had no cause to tell him to leave." Mary picked up the fallen chair and set it soundly on the floor. She gave the fire a violent poke with the stick, sending sparks flying dangerously in all directions.

Luke made no reply. He walked around the room three or four times, pushing his hands through his hair, picking things up from the table, putting them down. Finally he stopped in front of Mary and looked straight at her.

"Mary, if we was to get married I'd come to live here where you like it so much. You and Henry is here by yourselves. Bears and foxes and wolves ain't the only wild animals you got to be afeard of. Them Indians ain't the only folks that come visiting unexpected. I know them. They won't harm you none. But you're a girl alone and when the men up at the Corners get sitting around the fire in Hazen's store, drinking and thinking about that, some of them maybe ain't gonna stop at the thinking.

"Mebbe you can take care of Sim. You know him and he's not quite a man growed; but some of the men with the same kind of idea is a lot bigger and older and maybe a lot stronger. It scares me, Mary."

"But it maybe is not the very best reason for getting married, Luke."

"Mebbe it ain't the worst, either." He smiled suddenly. "You know it ain't the only reason for me asking, Mary."

"Please, Luke." She turned away. "I will not marry you. I will marry no man. Not now. Not ever."

Luke took her by the shoulder and spun her around. "Mary, you can't marry a deader."

Mary drew in her breath sharply. "I am not meant for marrying." Her voice was choked. "I... I am not meant for living in houses all closed and full of smoke. I am not meant for a life of spinning and weaving. I am not meant for living in a forest that shadows the world with its great dark and swallows what is most precious."

"Then what are you meant for, for God's sake?" Luke began pacing again.

"I am meant for the hills where my feet know where to walk, and to those hills I will go as soon as ever I can earn my passage money home."

They glared at each other. "And anyway, Luke," Mary added scathingly, "I could not marry a lad who paces and paces and paces his life away!"

Luke threw himself through the door and out into the night. An instant later he was back for his coat. There was rage in his eyes. "Pacing's better than lying mouldering in a grave," he shouted. He slammed the door.

In a blind fury Mary cleared away the uneaten food and the dishes and set the kettle back on the hearth.

From the loft came the sound of sobbing. Mary clambered up the ladder. Henry was sitting up in bed. In the moonlight Mary could see the tears streaming down his face. He had been crying for some time, silently, into his bedclothes. His face was swollen and his body was shaking with sobs.

"Henry! Do not weep so." Mary put her arms tightly around him and rocked him back and forth. Through his sobs Henry managed to stammer, "A-a-are you g-going away?"

"I am not! It will be so much time before I have earned the money to buy my passage home, you will be grown with bairns of your own before I do. Och, my wee *uan*, do not weep." She held him close, crooning to him and rocking him until his sobs subsided and he fell asleep.

She went to bed then but she did not sleep. Luke's harsh words, "can't marry a deader", refused to leave her, and that night the snow blew through the chinks in the logs and Duncan's voice that was not Duncan's voice cried on the wind, "cold, cold, so cold, Mairi, I am so-o co-o-old!" She lay all night with the cover wound around her head to keep from hearing it.

CHAPTER XIV

There Is No Summer

The trouble, when it came, was not what Luke had warned about. It began with the children. One morning, early in June, Sarah Yardley did not come to school. This did not alarm Mary. But she noticed the furtive glances darting around the room and the haste with which Sarah Pritchett began her ciphering lessons.

Two days later Polly and Joey Heaton were missing, then the four Bradley children and Matilda Hesse. By this time Mary knew something was wrong. Sarah would not look at her. She fidgeted with her sash, she dropped her bit of chalk. She jumped at every sound. But she would only say, "So many are ill. There is so much croup among the children and so much quinsy." Henry wouldn't look at her either and said only, "I dunno," when she asked him what was happening.

She went to see Patty. "She will tell me," she thought.

"Patty ain't here." Hannah Openshaw's usually harried but jovial face was guarded. Mary walked slowly back up the road. Something was clearly very wrong.

Luke told her. He came that evening with a partridge for Henry's board. He had not come to visit or to read in the month and a half since Simeon had behaved so badly, since he himself had again asked Mary to marry him. He had become as distant as before Henry's near drowning. Mary was too proud and too unhappy to try to make things right. On this evening, though, she stopped him to ask why the children were not coming to school.

"It's the things you been telling them," he answered bluntly. "It's about them terrible critters you say you see, and ghosts, and how you can see what's gonna happen, and about Sim disappearing. You got them yonkers scared out of their wits thinking you can put spells onto them. And what's more, you got a parcel of their mothers and a couple of their fathers thinking the same. Here it is June and it's too cold to plant. Some of the trees have lost their leaves. It's almost like winter again—just the way you said. You got to see how that scares folks. A whole lot of others think you're a real loony and they ain't so sure they want you teaching their children."

"I did not make the cold come, Luke, and I have invented nothing," Mary cried passionately. "Well, almost nothing...." She had remembered the story of the eighty-seven-year-old sheep who had started life as a schoolboy. "But those *critters* are not here to bother the bairns. I told you that. They...." Mary took a deep breath. "They have dwelt too long among their own rocks, in their own burns and lochs, those old ones. They cannot pick up their belongings in a scrap of linen and sail off across the western ocean. But ghosts, Luke, they stay among us for good or ill, here as there, rooted to the places where they lived. How can you believe I invented ghosts?" She stopped, remembering something else he had said. "And what do the children say about Simeon? I cannot make Simeon disappear. Henry, do you think I am a witch who can make folk disappear?"

Henry had been sitting, all the while, on the stool by the fire. He looked at Mary, his grey eyes big and dark, rubbing his hands nervously back and forth along the rough cloth of his breeches.

"I don't know," he whispered.

"Do you think I can put spells on folk?"

"That's what you says in school." The whisper was barely audible.

"Truly I do so, Henry, but it is to keep those big lads behaving themselves. Do you think I would ill-wish the children? Henry, how can you? And whatever do you mean, loony?"

A smile flickered across Luke's broad face. "It means crazy. Crazy people laugh like loons, I guess."

"Do they? Do I?"

"Maybe not. Mary, why don't you take a stick to the big lads, like anybody else. Don't talk loony to them."

Mary did not reply. The three of them sat in uncomfortable silence, looking at the fire, looking anywhere but at one another. Mary felt more alone and farther from home than at any time since she had come to Upper Canada. "I think maybe you'd best talk to Dan Pritchett," said Luke.

"Why?"

"Well, Dan's kind of sensible. You might tell him as how you was inventing stories to keep the big fellers in line and you're sorry."

"I only invented one story and three spells and I am not sorry." Mary sprang from her chair. "If the children—or anyone—think I am a witch who can make folk disappear—if they think I can make Simeon disappear—but why do they think like this about Simeon? Where is he?"

"Didn't you know Sim ain't around?"

"Ain't around?" she repeated stupidly.

"He's run off, I expect."

"Run off?"

"He ain't the first feller to cut and run under the circumstances," said Luke drily, "but he ain't here to show himself to the children you been telling them spells to. So you might better go talk to Dan." Luke stood up. With a curt "Good night," he left.

After he had gone Henry went to his loft at once, and very quietly. Mary went to sit by Duncan's grave. It was as cold as November and the wind was coming up from the east. She didn't care.

"Duncan," she said softly, "did they call you loony, too? Do they not feel their mothers and fathers, their dead children, whispering through the grass? Does the laughter of their loved ones not cling to their lofts and sing at their hearths?"

There was only the wind in the trees for an answer.

That night the voice was louder, more insistent.

June was almost over but the days were still growing colder. There was ice along the edges of the bay and the creek. Heavy frost had come again and most of the plants that had sprung up along the shore and roadsides had frozen and turned black. It was too late for planting. Julia Colliver told Mary that Sam said there'd be no flour to mill for next winter. They were going to have to scout around down the St. Lawrence river to buy it.

"You're a queer one, telling us all this was gonna happen. You sure troubled a lot of folks with your talk. It's a good thing, I say, the cows and hens and sheep ain't bothered by the things you say."

Besides Henry, only the Morrissay and Colliver children were still at school. Then Dan Pritchett came one morning to tell Mary that she would not be needed any longer, that Sarah could manage alone.

"But Miss Pritchett is no different now from the way she was when I began." Pushed by her unhappiness—and her need—Mary spoke out boldly.

"All the same, she can manage," Dan replied firmly, although he looked uncomfortable about having to tell her and he did not linger to talk about it. Mary remembered bitterly Martha Pritchett saying, "Nothing I can ever do for you can repay...," and Dan himself: "Right glad to be doing some kind of good turn." She was too proud to mention those words, too proud to argue with him.

Bewildered by Dan's action, and afraid, Mary did her afternoon's work, fed Henry his supper, and went in the dark and cold to sit again by Duncan's grave.

"How will I manage now, *mo gràdach*? How can I stay here? How can I pay rent and earn money for my passage home if I am not to teach the children? Och, Duncan, he is unkind. They are all unkind."

"Unkind, unkind," echoed the wind.

"I cannot go to Dan Pritchett and tell him I have been making stories and spells when I have not," she thought stubbornly. "Surely he can understand that. Surely he knows I am not daft."

Patty understood. She came the next morning as Mary was standing in the creek washing her clothes, her feet blue with cold, her face red from exertion. Henry was walking slowly around and around the house, running a stick up and down the logs, causing Mary's aching head to jump with pain with every rattling sound.

Patty began to wring the clothes. "I'm right sorry about the young 'uns having to quit your school. Ma took Mose home on account of that silly Annie Heaton. She said stupid things about you putting marks on her children. She's an Irisher and she's always saying things like that. You'd think a woman as big as Ma would have more sense in her than to listen to the likes of Annie Heaton, but she don't. Only Phoebe Morrissay's willing to keep on, but of course those children ain't gonna come without the others—they wanted a holiday, them others, if you ask me! And look how they got their elders hopping!"

"Did you... do you believe I would put spells on folk?" Mary's voice was hesitant.

"Naw. I don't believe no one can make spells, nor make the weather go bad neither. I know you ain't had nothing to do with that."

Mary straightened abruptly. "Do folk say I have?" She snatched up the shirt she had been pounding on a stone and hung onto it, dripping icy water down the front of her blouse. "How could I?" she cried.

"That's what I said."

"But do they believe that? Do they?" Mary threw her hair back from her face and jumped to the bank. She grabbed Patty by her arm. "What do they say, Patty? What do they say?"

"Whoa." Patty stepped back. Henry's shirt fell to the ground. "Well...." She look embarrassed. "Well, they say that if you can do the things you tell the children you can do—turn them into sheep— and see when people are going to die—you might, you just might, mind you, have something to do with there being no summer. You did go round and say there wasn't gonna be one. You know how people talk. They just talk and...oh, Mary, I wish you wouldn't of told no one you seen the frozen gardens in your dream."

"It wasn't a dream and I thought folk would want to know," said Mary miserably.

"Here, come on." Patty picked up the pile of wet laundry. "You're soaking wet. You'll catch your death. I don't see why you gotta wash clothes by trampling around on 'em in this freezing water. Why don't you wash 'em in a tub like the rest of us? Ma says why do you have to...never mind, let's get us something hot to drink, I'm like to die of cold standing here."

Seated by the fire, drinking the hot coffee Patty had made, Mary was suddenly overcome by her kindness.

"When your mother said you were not home the day I came to see you, I thought you did not want to see me any more. You have not been here in weeks."

"It wasn't I didn't want to see you." Patty paused. "It was something else. It...." She gulped. "I'm having a baby."

"A baby?"

"Yep. You know them little human beings that cries so much and makes so much mess but nuzzles up to you so's you can't never say no to them."

"But I do not see... I mean I did not know...."

"Simeon Anderson."

"Simeon? Are you to marry Simeon? But I thought...."

"You thought I was sweet on Luke on account of I told you that. Well, mebbe I was but it ain't Luke helped make this baby I'm gonna have." Patty's cheeks had turned scarlet. "It was the night Luke and I come busting in when you was gonna take after Sim with your knife. I felt pretty low seeing Luke looking at you like you was his girl. I guess I didn't much care when Sim got himself all over me and... and I guess we made a baby. Ma's in a terrible state and Pa swears every time he looks at me. He says he'll skin Sim alive if he ever catches him. Anyways I figure I done all the crying about it I'm gonna and," she finished disconsolately, "it don't much look like I'm gonna marry nobody. Sim's run off."

A vision of Patty in her blue dress cooking at the Anderson fire came to Mary. In the vision the cabin had become tidy and cheerful. Patty was smiling. John was coming through the door, Luke and Henry were sitting at the table. They looked like a family. The vision faded leaving Mary feeling bereft, left out. She did not want to tell Patty about it, but at the same time she wanted to comfort her friend. "Do not trouble yourself, Patty, it will come right for you."

Patty's big eyes grew bigger. Then she smiled. "I don't believe you know that but, Mary, when you say it so nice, I do feel better."

After she had left, Mary found Henry and went at once to the Collivers'. She needed to be busy. Although she knew it wasn't reasonable, the thought of Patty and Luke getting married made her feel very alone.

Three days later Patty came to tell Mary she was going to marry John Anderson. "I'd as soon have John as Sim," she said. "Sooner, I guess."

"But you...but Luke," Mary blurted out. She had been so sure the vision meant Luke.

"But but." Patty poked her plump finger at Mary. "But Luke ain't for me. Luke ain't cared a fiddle-stick for any but you since he first clapped eyes on you. Julia Colliver told me he was like someone with a rare treasure to be fixed the day he brung you to her when you first come to the Corners. I figured, when you told me you wasn't fixing to marry, that I'd have a chance with Luke. The night Sim was offering to bother you and I seen the look on Luke's face I knew I hadn't. He ain't for me, Mary Urkit. Whether you wants to know about it or whether you doesn't, he's yours."

Mary could not respond to those words. She was doing her best to ignore the surge of relief she felt.

"Getting married is special and we must have something special to celebrate," she cried. She went to the cupboard and took from it the packet of real tea Phoebe Morrissay had given her at Christmas, and a honeycomb left from last summer that Henry had found in the woods. "I expect it is not a marriage for you to rejoice in." Mary put the tea in the kettle.

"Why not? John's a good man. He's had a hard time. Lydia Anderson was a sad woman and none too strong. It was powerful hard on her losing all them babies, but it was hard on John too, and with her taking to the drink like that. I like him. He likes me. He'll be good to me and the baby. We'll do well enough together. I...I've gone along up to the Andersons' to live. We'll get married when preacher comes in August."

Mary was too astounded to be polite. "Patty, how can you be this way? You just let things happen to you, whatever comes along, and you do not seem to mind."

"Mind? What's the good of minding? This is how things turned out. I just got to make the best of them. What good would I do screaming and shouting or throwing myself every which way?" She smiled broadly, and Mary, who had been so cold and unhappy, felt warm.

After Patty had left Mary went to look for Henry. She could find him nowhere. He was not at the Openshaws'. He was not at the Pritchetts'. Mrs. Colliver told her he had gone fishing with Matthew.

Matthew came back before Mary was finished with her work. Relieved, she hurried home to make supper for Henry, promising herself she would not scold him. But Henry had not come home.

CHAPTER XV
Duncan

Mary waited until well after dark for Henry. But she knew he was not coming, she knew where he had gone—and she went there to bring him home. There was snow on the ground again; the road was firm and it was as cold as January under the bright stars. But Mary hardly noticed. Stolidly she tramped the five miles to the Anderson homestead.

She was afraid. The voice called to her unceasingly now and she could not bear to be alone. She needed Henry with her. She was afraid, too, that Dan might make her leave her house, and she was afraid of the neighbours who had seemed so warm and friendly in the winter. She pushed open the Andersons' door without knocking and there was Patty standing by the fire. John was coming in the back door from the shed, Luke and Henry were sitting at the table. The room looked as she had already seen it—neat and inviting.

"Henry," cried Mary, "it's time you were coming home!"

Henry stared down at the table. Mary crossed the room to stand over him. "Henry!" Her voice shook. "Henry, I was so worried. Do come away home now."

Henry looked desperately at Luke from the corner of his eye. Luke glanced towards his father. "Didn't you tell Mary you was coming home?" John demanded.

Henry shook his head.

"Henry, that ain't right."

Henry said nothing. Mary was desperate. "Tell him he must come, Luke."

"Mary...." Luke's tone was without emotion. "It looks like Henry wants to come home."

"But he lives with me. You brought him to live with me. He needs me." A lump *would* come in Mary's throat, though she swallowed hard against it.

"Do you want to go with Mary, Henry?" Luke looked at his young brother. Neither Patty nor John said anything. Henry shook his head almost imperceptibly.

"I guess he don't." Luke's voice was softer. "Come along, Mary. Patty'll fix you some coffee and grub."

"I do not want coffee. I want only to take Henry home."

"Mary, he don't want to come." He was beginning to sound angry. "Henry don't want to come.

He's scared. He figures you've made bad things happen, no matter what we say."

"What did you tell him? Did you say I made Sim disappear?"

"Don't be stupid. I told him Sim run off, only he can't figure it that way."

"Why didn't you tell him?" Mary whirled to confront Patty.

John moved forward. "Patty's had enough trouble without we should get the children all riled up about it. Mary, it's time Henry was coming home now that Patty's here and we've got things in order."

"But the children are riled up. They are riled up about *me*. They are riled up so that I may not teach them and I will have to give up my house and now even Henry has run to seek protection against me. Does that not count for anything?"

"I guess you might say the whole neighbourhood is riled up about you," said Luke drily.

"Luke, don't be mean." Patty took a step towards Mary.

"Luke," Mary pleaded, "Luke, if we were to marry could Henry come back to me?"

For almost a minute the only sound in the room was the crackling fire. Luke's face went red. He slammed his fist on the table. "No!" he shouted; then, in barely lowered tones, he let loose his frustrations. "I guess there's reasons the neighbourhood's riled up about you, Mary Urkit. You stirred up a lot of things in these parts with your talk of ghosts and seeing things before they happen. Riled! You sure got me riled. You got us all going like a fife-and-drum marching band with your queer talk and your soft ways. You ain't interested in marrying me. And Henry don't need you now; you're too dang-blasted proud to say it but you need Henry, though God in heaven knows the only person you got any room for is that useless dead cousin of yours. All he did last I seen him was mope around like a big black shadow. He got himself dead but he ain't changed much. He's still a black shadow. Henry's well out of that place. I don't want nothing to do with it and I don't want nothing to do with you, neither. I wish you *would* go home, where you want to go so bad, and take the shadow with you—and I expect I might just help you do it. I got some money put by to get me a parcel of land, and maybe I'll give it to you so's you can buy your way.''

Luke stopped. He was breathing hard in an effort to control himself.

Mary recoiled as though she had been struck. She stumbled across the room and out the door. ''Mary!'' Patty called after her. She did not stop. She ran all the way home.

She sat through the night by the fire, getting up only to put another log on. She did not spin. She did not eat. She did not go to bed. Luke and Henry were both gone. As the night wore on there was only that voice that was Duncan but was not Duncan, like a wild song growing louder and louder, until it came at her from every corner of the house. ''Come, Mairi, come. Mairi, come. Come, Mairi.''

She could fight it no longer. Towards dawn she got up and went down to the big grey rock by the edge of the black water. It was snowing lightly and ice had formed in winded ruffles along the shore.

The marsh marigolds and bullrushes that had been so bright in the brief warm spell early in May had all gone. The few birds had gone into the deep woods for shelter. All was cold and silent and strange.

"Mairi, come." Duncan's voice was soft, cajoling now. She sighed. Slowly she put off her shawl, pulled her shift over her head, untied her skirt and let it slip from her. She took off her moccasins and her stockings. She stood naked in the snow. She did not feel the cold. She reached around and unbraided her hair. It fell like a black mantle around her shoulders.

Softly she began to sing in Gaelic a song for the dying, and as she sang she stepped off the rock into the bay. She walked out until she stood waist-deep in the water.

"I am coming, *mo gràdach*. I am coming to be where you are." She looked down into the black water and there she saw Duncan lying beneath the surface, his dead white face turned towards her, his black hair floating around him like the fronds of a fern. His eyes were open, his hands were outstretched, waiting.

Mary stared at the apparition. It was as real as though Duncan's body itself floated there. She closed her eyes. She opened them. The apparition was still there. She understood, at last. And came to herself.

"Duncan, you did this!" she accused him. "You drowned yourself in this water, and you would take me too. But I will not follow you to the grave." Frantically she turned and began to push her way through the water towards the shore. She stopped and turned back. The image was still there. She leaned down. She could see her own distraught reflection superimposed on the image of Duncan. She took a deep, shuddering breath. "Duncan *dubh*, in death as in life you would have bound me to you. It cannot be. I will not come. I will do my best to forgive you and I wish you safe journey to the land of the dead." She reached down and gently, as though Duncan were there in body, she put out her hands and closed his eyelids. She said for him the blessing of the dead and waded back to the shore.

The ends of her hair were stiff with ice, her teeth were clattering, she was blue and covered with goose-bumps. She grabbed her clothes and dashed into the house. She stirred up the fire, drank the hot water that was in the kettle, dried and dressed herself, and wrapped around her all the shawls and blankets she had.

When she had warmed to the point where she could begin to think, the thoughts charged at her like an assaulting army: "It is true, I have been as one daft since I came here—since before that. I knew. I did know that you were dead. Inside myself I knew that you had drowned yourself. It was on the ship, it was when Kirsty Mackay went under the sea. I knew it but I did not want to know, I would not let myself know—and now I have lost so much." She saw again Henry's frightened face by the light of the Andersons' fire—and Luke's angry one. Tears spilled down her cheeks and fell on her clenched hands. But the thoughts did not stop.

"We were as one, it is what we both thought— did we think about it at all? Reflections, our mams said, and we could not see, not you, not me, that life could be without the other. But—'' Mary had a flash of understanding that made her gasp and spring to her feet. "But Duncan," she cried aloud, "I did go on without you! Even at home after you had gone. But you could not go on without me. You turned from me for four years—four long years. When you wanted to die, then you called. You wanted me to die with you." She sank back into her chair. "What you did was not my fault," she whispered, "it was not. Luke was right. A shadow, he said." Wonderingly she repeated it aloud. "A shadow. Alive and dead, you were like a shadow. And I thought I could not manage life without you. I thought you were so strong because you were beautiful and exciting. Time was I would follow you anywhere. When you called me I could not believe evil of you. I thought it must be a devil. Mam was right."

The realization of what had happened struck her anew. "But not into that other world I would not follow. Duncan, it was not strong to drown yourself so, it was evil to come after me. It was evil that you would take Henry because he was my comfort. That was not love, Duncan." She put her head into her hands and wept.

In time her tears ceased to flow and she sat, subdued but peaceful, wrapped in her old shawl, the blankets from her and Henry's beds, and the fine wool shawl Mrs. Grant had given her the night she had left the glen. "To be married in," the old woman had said.

"Better to warm myself in it today than be buried in it tomorrow," Mary thought ruefully. "I will not

201

be buried now for a long time, but I have taken a queer stitch in my life and the Lord knows what will become of me.'' She stood and stretched her stiff legs and back.

Outside the snow had stopped falling. The day was cold and clear. Mary went down to stand again on the big grey rock. A breeze was moving along the water so that it lapped against the frozen shore, making little icy curls. The water itself was transparent, revealing every twig, every stone beneath. A school of minnows darted past under the surface. There was nothing else.

Mary smiled. She left the shore and walked up past the house and across the road. She stopped by Duncan's grave.

''I am going into the forest now,'' she said. Without hesitating she walked on until she could see nothing in any direction but trees. There she stopped. And stood. And wondered.

She had not expected silence. At the edge of the forest and in the clearings the sound of the wind soughing, sighing through the tops of the great pines, was everywhere and almost constant. Here, deep in the evergreen forest itself, there was no sound, the light was as dim as it must be under the sea. All around were the huge tree trunks, gigantic columns hundreds of years old, rising beyond where her eyes could find their tops, columns far enough apart for an ox-cart to pass between. There were no small trees, no underbrush this deep in the woods—not enough sunlight reached the forest floor for them to survive; only the giants growing out of a carpet of pine needles, soft and dry. There was no sign of the snow that clung to the ground outside. Nor of the cold.

Gradually Mary unclenched her fists, her jaws, the muscles in her neck, and then her whole body. She listened for the sounds of the forest as she had once listened for the sounds of a fairy hill. And she heard the silence.

After a long time, she sat down on the soft pine needles with her back against a tree and let the silence settle into her. In time she heard little sounds—the fluttering and cheeping of small birds in the lower branches of the evergreens, a wood-pecker tap-tapping against a dead trunk near the edge of the woods, small animals scurrying round the roots, scampering up into knot-holes. She lifted her eyes towards the treetops, where a glint of sun had shot through an opening like a diamond spar-kling in a dark mine.

"I feel no spirits of people gone," she thought, and remembered Luke telling her that no people had lived in these forests ever. Even the Indians had never settled here, they had merely traded and trav-elled the lakes and along the shores of the island. There had always been only the trees.

"And the water—and the ice." Mary thought about the heartbeat in the bay's sudden freezing. She thought about the forest. She ran her hand along the smooth pine needles and knew that this new land had reached out to her. She leaned back against the tree, smiling.

CHAPTER XVI
Luke

Mary emerged from the woods half an hour later feeling she had been blessed. All the world seemed to reflect her feelings. The stones in the road sparkled under the bright mid-morning sun, the exposed tree roots had taken on a honeyed sheen. The wind no longer seemed to moan or cry. It sounded to Mary like a hymn.

At that moment, Luke appeared from around the corner of her house. His head was down and he did not see her.

"Luke," Mary called.

He started, looked up, and ran towards her. She ran forward to meet him. He clutched her shoulders. "You...you didn't. You're all right." His voice was strained and his face was grey. "Oh, Mary." His fingers tightened on her arms.

"Luke, what is it?"

"I thought…. Mary, I…."

"Luke!" Mary knew. "I did not. I meant to, but I could not. Och, *mo gràdach*!" She threw her arms around him and they hugged each other until Luke stopped shaking.

Disentangling himself, he drew his sleeve across his face and looked at her, fear still dark in his eyes but the colour beginning to return to his cheeks.

"Mary, I didn't mean to say all those miserable things. I was mad, I was *so* mad. I only got cooled down a little while back. I got to thinking what I'd said about you being crazy—I don't think that! Then I got to thinking what happened to Duncan Cameron and—and I was so scared! But you're all right. And I don't want you to go away. But I will give you the money I've got saved if it will make you happy."

"Luke, you have no need to give me anything. I have been so unkind to you."

"No, you haven't. You've been powerful kind. It's us who wasn't. You would have gone home lickerty-split when you found out Duncan was dead only I fetched you to care for the baby, then you stayed to tend Henry, then I brung him to you after when all you wanted was to be by yourself. Then Sim…well, Henry got scared. He got to thinking you could make him disappear and he didn't want to."

"And I will do it if ever I find him acting like Sim!"

"I never met anybody like you before." Luke stared fixedly at a spot somewhere just above Mary's head. "It's what I told you—I never give a thought to marrying before you come," he said slowly and this time he did look at her. "But I couldn't help it. It wasn't like they say about getting sweet on someone, it was like looking at someone I was supposed to be with, and I wasn't even all that surprised. It just felt natural and I guess I figured you'd be bound to feel the same sooner or later. I guess I been pestering. I'm no better than Sim when it comes right down to it."

"Luke! You are *not* like Sim, not the smallest mote of dust like Sim. Luke, if you still want I will marry you now. I will, really."

"No," said Luke, "you don't have to say that. I'm just glad you're all right. You *are* all right, aren't you?" He paused. "Mary, something's changed in you. Mary! You been in the woods!"

"I have." Mary was suddenly very tired. "Luke, I will tell you. I will tell you about going into the forest and…and other things, but I think I must go to bed now. Please go home. Go home and tell Henry that if he is good I will not make him disappear."

Luke grinned. "I will tell him what I should have told him in the first place, that Sim run off because he said too many bad things and was ashamed for 'em."

"God would smite you for such a lie, Luke Anderson," Mary said severely, but the corner of her mouth twitched.

Luke insisted on walking with her to her front door, said good morning, and started off. He hadn't taken more than a few steps when he came back.

"There's something changed about this place, too." His face was puzzled.

"There is."

Luke waited for her to continue. When she didn't, he looked around once more, said goodbye again, and left.

Mary didn't sleep and she was still not hungry. She ate a corncake, drank a cup of root coffee, and swept out her house, letting the knowledge of what had happened—to Duncan, to herself—settle deep into her. At noon she went to the Collivers' to see to the lambs.

Charity Hazen was looking out for her as she came up the road. "Hey, Mary Urkit, there's mail for you. Feller named Macleod on his way to the Crossing left it for you, said he'd be back in a week and a half to look you up." She handed Mary a small parcel.

"Sandy Macleod from home," Mary breathed. "Sandy Macleod, cousin to Johnny Fraser." She looked at the small parcel wrapped in blue linen. She held it against her cheek for a moment and inhaled the scent of the cloth. She swallowed hard. "Thank you," she told Mrs. Hazen and tucked the parcel away in the pocket she wore inside her skirt. She wanted to wait to open it when she was in her own house alone.

All afternoon, as she worked in the barn with Zeke and Arn Colliver feeding and comforting a pair of orphaned lambs, she reached now and then into her pocket to touch the parcel. When at last she was back by her own hearth, she took it out. Trembling, she cut the stitches that held it fast. Inside was a letter folded around another parcel, this one wrapped in white linen. She put the letter with the scrap of blue cloth and unwound the white linen to reveal a further wrapping, and another, until at last, shining up at her from its nest of cloth, lay the Urquhart cairngorm brooch.

Through the tears that would come, the peaty-brown colour of the cairngorm glistened like a Highland burn in the spring sun, under the dappled shade of rowans and alders. Mary could almost hear Duncan's impatient, little-boy voice calling, "Mairi, Mairi, come quick! There's a fish, a fish for us." She blinked. The image was gone and the cairngorm lay there in her lap.

The letter was from her father. He told her that in the year that she had been gone, Uncle Davie and Aunt Jean and the boys had arrived home safely. He also said that her sister Jeannie and Johnny Fraser had married, but that the baby that had been going to come soon after had been lost, and that Jeannie could have no more.

"I will have no descendants unless they be yours," he wrote. "If you do not marry, you must do with the brooch what you feel is best." He closed by telling her that both he and her mother were well. The letter was not long nor was it obviously a loving letter. It was not James Urquhart's way to write such a letter. His gift and his few spare words told Mary poignantly that he loved her and that he wanted either for her to have children to leave the brooch to, or for her to sell it and come home. She sat for another long night by the fire, dozing only now and again, moving to stir the fire and, once, to make herself tea.

She was not grieving. She was thinking—and remembering; remembering home, the fragrance of the golden whin and broom, the roses and the purple heather. She was remembering that she had once told Duncan when they were children, "When I am old, I will lie myself down on the hill and my roots will push themselves into the earth and I will sleep." And Duncan had said, "And I will be there, too." And she had agreed, for they were not to be parted.

"But you lie here," she murmured," beside the dark forest, and though the black shade of you called me, I would not go that far with you. Your shade is at rest now, too. I can go home, if I wish." The picture of Luke came to mind, his eyes dark with fear. "Someone I was supposed to be with," he had said.

She went to bed, her head full of thoughts of Luke, and when she woke in the morning she knew what she was going to do. She bathed herself in the creek, scolding her shivering body—"I could all but drown myself in the icy water without a groan or a sigh—now I surely can bathe in it." She put on her clean shift, her good red-and-blue-checked skirt, her clean white linen blouse, her stockings, and her shoes. She combed her hair down smooth and straight, put her warm plaid around her shoulders, pinned the cairngorm at her shoulder, and took from the cupboard shelf the neatly folded length of creamy white cloth she had woven as the first instalment on her passage home.

Journeying through the woods was a great deal faster than by the road. Mary reached the Anderson homestead in less than an hour. The day was warmer than days had been for weeks and Luke, his father, and Henry were out planting pumpkins in a last effort to battle the wintry summer. Mary stood at the edge of the field watching them make neat rows with their hoes until Henry looked up and saw her. He started to smile, then an expression of shame and self-consciousness crossed his face. He looked away.

"Henry," Mary called, "Henry, you cannot for ever not speak to me because you have been foolish. Come you here."

Henry stood up, and slowly, as though each step were painful, crossed the small field. Mary knelt down so that she could talk to him at his own level.

"Well then," she said, "if I were to touch you, would you disappear, do you think?"

Henry was looking at his feet. "No," he whispered.

"What then do you think might happen to you?"

"I don't know."

"Are you afraid to look at me?"

"Yes."

"Henry, I am afraid about something I mean to do. If I have the courage to do this thing I fear, will you look at me then?"

Henry raised his eyes in surprise. "Not yet, laddie, for I have not done it yet." She stood up. She drew a deep breath.

"Luke," she called. "Luke Anderson. I have come courting and I have brought you a gift." She held out the folded length of cloth.

Luke gaped at her from the other side of the field. He did not move.

Mary was trembling. Her hands had broken out in a sweat. She took a few steps.

"It is in my mind," she said, "that it would make a fine wedding shirt. It is not perfect but I have woven it myself. If you refuse my courting, Luke, I can do no less than you and tell you the gift is yours, all the same."

Still Luke stood motionless on his side of the field. Mary stood on hers, fearing that her knees would fail her. Then Luke let out a whoop, bounded across the field, and swept her into a hug that lifted her right off her feet.

"This ain't no wrestling match, son," shouted his father, laughing, and Patty, standing in the doorway, teased, "Luke, you'll ruin the beautiful cloth!"

"But what's the thing you're afraid of?" demanded Henry.

"It was not really a thing." Mary moved a small space away from Luke. "It was Luke. Will you look at me, now?"

"You're afeard of Luke?" Henry was incredulous.

"Sometimes I am afraid of you."

"Of me? I'm not afraid of you...oh." Henry's face reddened.

Later when they were walking hand in hand back through the woods, Mary told Luke about seeing Duncan in the water and about her time in the forest. "Then you came," she said.

"Were you really afraid of me?" asked Luke.

"I was. It was my pride, Luke." She sighed ruefully. "I think now I should not have been. I have remembered Mrs. Grant's prophecy."

"Mary, see here—"

Firmly Mary reached up and put her hand over his mouth. "It is time for you to see here. Listen.

'Twice will you refuse your destiny, twice will you seek it before you embrace it as your own.' Mrs. Grant, who has the two sights, told me that the night I left home. I thought she meant that it was my destiny to be a seer and a healer and that I had refused it twice—once when I did not tell you about seeing you carrying Henry before he fell and once when I did not warn of the Pritchetts' fire the day I hid in the privy. Then, when I was coming through the woods for you, I knew *you* were the destiny she meant. But when I saw you in the field, you looked so far away and so stern all I could think was that you had said, more than once, you would not marry me after all—and I was afraid.''

''But I am going to marry you.'' Luke's eyes were shining. ''Mary, I been thinking. You told me to watch out for Ma in the snow—and I got to tell you I did try—just in case you wasn't as loony as I figured. And it did give me a turn that you ran all the way from the Collivers' in time to save Henry from drowning. Now you tell me how it was you near drowned yourself—'' His hand tightened on hers. ''And how you seen Duncan in the water. I seen for myself how peaceful it was there afterwards when you went home from being in the woods. Well, I've been thinking there must be something to what you say about all that. We just ain't raised to think that way. I see the birds and the trees and the lake—and the land to be cleared and ploughed. I guess you see all sorts of things I don't. Mebbe I wish I could, too, but I don't think so. I wonder if sometimes you ain't just so caught up in looking for your ghosts and fairies and strange critters that you miss some of what I see.''

Mary looked solemnly at his open face. "It is no easy thing to understand. But I do understand this. I came to this place when Duncan called and now I know you were the one here waiting for me. I cannot go home without you.

"And there is something else. Here where I have been so afraid and so sure I did not belong—teaching, working with Julia Colliver, living with Henry, being with you—I am more a part of your neighbourhood than I ever was of my own in my own hills. My heart can never truly leave those hills, Luke. I know I must live with that sadness but I know that I do not have to live as though burdened by a heavy cloak soaked in rain. I can wear the burden lightly because I chose both the sadness and the joy."

Shyly, self-consciously, Mary and Luke put their arms around each other and kissed in the privacy of the deep woods.

They agreed to be married in August, with John and Patty and four other couples, when the preacher came again to the district. They decided to live at Hawthorn Bay. Henry was going to live with them. Sarah Pritchett gave them the house, the lot, and twenty acres across the road for a wedding present. "Part of the land Dan owns is mine as my Loyalist grant from the King, and I want you to have this piece of it. I think you're a brave young woman, Mary Urquhart, to hold strong with your own ways when all were against you." She twisted the sash of her dress until it was like a spring as she talked, but she persevered, and when she had finished she handed Mary the deed to the property. Mary and

Luke thanked her together and promised to "hold strong" with both their ways.

Owena brought Mary a handsome deerskin dress. "It is for walking among the trees," she said. She had a pair of moccasins for Luke.

Word had come from pedlars from New York and New England that there was no summer anywhere that year—"eighteen-hundred-and-freeze-to-death", they were calling it back in Vermont. Whichever of Mary's neighbours had harboured the notion that she might have caused the bad weather sheepishly relinquished it.

Few people mentioned that Mary had predicted the weather. And it was suddenly remembered that Simeon Anderson had always been a "wild one, too fond of his whisky, too loose with his words".

Dan gave a small parcel of land for a school, and the community elders—Dan, Sam Colliver, Jim Morrissay, Hiram Openshaw, and Liam Hennessy—asked Mary to teach the children. Gravely she accepted.

The wedding was to be by the creek near the mill. The wedding feast was to be at the Collivers'. Mrs. Colliver would listen to no refusals. "Luke brung you here in the first place for me to take care of, and seeing you safely married's my job." Luke gave Mrs. Colliver his mother's rose-coloured silk wedding dress to be made over for Mary. He and his father bought cloth from the pedlar and made a special trip to Soames, to Micah Lambert, the tailor. Luke took with him Mary's hand-weaving for his shirt.

Mary insisted on spending the night before the wedding in her own house, making the room clean and bright, finding a few hardy leaves and a bit of blue chicory to put on her table, smooring the fire so that it would be set to come home to, and saying the words in Gaelic for good fortune in marriage. When all was done, before she put on the rose silk dress to wait for Luke to come for her in the horse and cart, she went across the road to Duncan's grave. She put a bouquet of dried rowan berries on it and said a small prayer. Then she knelt down to talk to him.

"It is well, Duncan," she said. "And it will be well, for it is meant to be. It is not the same here for me as it was at home—as it was not the same for you. The burns that rush so swiftly down our hillsides are not the creeks that wander through these deep woods. The high hills are not these low lands and the spirits of our rocks and hills and burns, the old ones who dwell in the unseen world, are not here.

"But we are not to grieve. The old ones came to our hills in the ancient times. It began somewhere. It began there long ago as it begins here now. We are the old ones here."

Mary fell silent. She stood up. Then she said again, very softly, "It is so, we are the old ones here." She went back to her house to dress for her wedding.